Nikolai

BLACK INC.
BOOK TWO

LISA MARIE RICE

CHAPTER

One

US Consulate, Naples
4th of July celebration

"Bruschetta, *signore?*" the roving waiter asked. Nikolai Garin suspiciously inspected the tray he was holding. The last thing he'd eaten—tried to eat—from a tray held by one of the waiters, he'd gagged, spit it out in his hand, and searched for a plant to drop the half-chewed remains of whatever it was in. He'd survived a thousand firefights, been stabbed, shot, run over, had had a partial parachute fail. And the greatest danger he'd ever faced had been some foodstuff offered by the United States Consulate in Naples, Italy. It had been that bad.

But the bruschetta being offered looked really good. Ripe tomatoes, juicy mozzarella slices, aromatic fresh basil leaves all gleaming with what looked like excellent extra virgin olive oil...yes.

His courage was rewarded. It was delicious. He was really hungry, since he'd skipped dinner last night going over the Consulate floor plans, breakfast had been a hurried espresso and lunch had been a tiny slice of cold pizza. So life owed him a decent bruschetta, or two, at the very least. He was going to treat himself to what was considered the best restaurant in Naples this evening, Il Terrazzone.

He turned around and rested his arms on the balustrade of the huge terrace of the Consulate. It had a spectacular view. The Consulate rested right on the famous bay, overlooked by the even more famous Mount Vesuvius. The sea sparkled, blue and green, hovercraft heading out to the islands of Capri and Ischia, or heading back in, all leaving a starry wake. The city was amazingly beautiful, ochre and brick-colored palazzos bright in the late afternoon sun.

A view to tug the heart.

Nikolai allowed himself to relax and enjoy the beauty. Beauty and work seldom went hand in hand for him. He specialized in bad guys and bad guys preferred shitholes, and God knows he'd been in plenty of them over the past years.

One of his last assignments had been overseeing an addition to the US Embassy in Pritzky, a broken city full of bullet holes and explosion craters, most walls bearing the black scorch marks of firebombs. At least three terrorist organizations had considered it a personal challenge to make the life of the construction workers impossible as they tried to build.

He was here in Naples consulting for the Consul General on a contract set to start in four days' time. The Consul had some serious concerns, but Nick had given himself a few days off before the contract started. While he was here, he was really enjoying the balmy weather, the beautiful architecture and the views. He hadn't eaten goat once, which was his culinary staple while in Pritzky, which amongst its many lousy attributes, was also a dry country.

He'd been very very happy to fly out, mission accomplished. Instead of flying home, which was a luxury service flat in London, he'd simply flown a couple of days early to Naples and was looking forward to just wandering around.

And now he was at work, easing into it gently, since the Consulate was closed today for the 4th of July. From the briefing with the Consul General over a secure line, he was beginning to suspect she had someone in-house who was selling secrets. And that someone was probably here.

He turned around lazily, back to the warm parapet, and studied the people who had been invited to the Consulate's annual 4th of July blowout, and who were going to be unhappy with at least some of the food. He scanned the huge terrace as if scanning enemy terrain. Scan a quarter of the field, blink to black, scan the next quarter...

And that's when he saw her. The most beautiful woman he'd ever seen.

She took his breath away. It took him a moment to even

get a general sense of her. Blue-black hair that hit her shoulders, shimmering like liquid when she moved. Eyes a piercing cobalt blue so intense they looked artificial, as if gemstones had replaced her eyes. And to continue that Snow White vibe, porcelain skin that stood out in a group of people who were all deeply sun tanned.

She had on a sharply tailored green linen top and linen skirt and looked sleekly elegant compared to the over-dressed ladies on the terrace.

Oh man. Nick had to get to know her. He'd spent the past months on mission with teammates and was sick of male company. With any luck, maybe his stay in Naples wouldn't be so bad, after all. He began drifting her way, but then hurried over when he saw what she was picking up off a tray.

LAUGHTER ROSE from the clusters of guests on the sunny terrace—rich expats, Italians with embassy ties, naval officers from the Sixth Fleet stationed in Naples, a scattering of local politicians eager to sip American champagne and be seen. The 4th of July in Naples was always one of the most lavish parties of the consular season, and George Stillwell should have been basking in the glow of it, surrounded by familiar colleagues, good food, privilege.

Everything he dreamed of when he sat for the series of exams to join the Foreign Service. He imagined exactly this. Cocktail parties on sunny terraces with the rich and powerful. Mingling with them, one of them.

Finally.

Instead, his gaze fixed on Nikolai Garin. The man hired by the Consul General, Caroline Munro, to do a security check on the Consulate because she suspected leaks.

Well...yes.

Yes, the Consulate had leaks. Very lucrative ones, too. His bank account was grateful. George was sure that the spyware he'd installed in Caroline Munro's cell was absolutely undetectable, but...damn. Garin was a part-owner of Black Inc., and no one's fool.

Garin stood against the balustrade of the terrace, back to the Bay, close enough to watch the crowd but far enough to be half-forgotten by it. He was observing everyone carefully, and George was grateful that he wasn't an imposing physical presence. It had made his life hell in high school, being thin and nerdy, but right now, Garin's gaze slid right past him without stopping.

Garin, instead, had presence. Lines of power surrounded him, even though he was utterly still. Not glad-handing himself around the terrace like everyone else.

He was a big man, with an athlete's build, made to attract attention, though he was clearly trying to be unnoticed.

He didn't move like the diplomats and businessmen and government servants circulating on the terrace. He had that terrible stillness George had only ever seen in predators—large cats pacing behind glass at the zoo when he was a child, eyes tracking prey across the walkway.

Garin shouldn't be here. An outsider, a...hired thug dressed in a suit. Caroline Munro, the Consul General, might be dazzled by him—Munro, with her crisp diction and upper-class schooling, who'd taken charge of the Consulate as though she'd been born to command palazzos instead of the Kansas plains. She's the one who chose Garin to investigate security at the Consulate, and she'd chosen the best.

George had tried to direct her, discreetly, to hire a second-tier company he knew would be unable to trace his app. But no. Munro went right to the top.

Munro tried to pass herself off as Everywoman, with her friendly manner and Midwestern accent. But George had taken a dive into her personal life. Her family ran something like 200 silos throughout the Midwest. And her father, instead of being a useless drunk like his father, was a canny investor. Munro had a trust fund of eight million dollars, though she tried to live within her salary. But Daddy always came through on Christmas and her birthday, with a new Mercedes, a diamond necklace, Apple stock.

She always pretended she was practical, no-nonsense, but she wasn't a self-made woman. Not at all.

And now she had hired Garin after announcing, that there were "security concerns."

Security concerns. George felt his throat tighten. If she only knew.

The air smelled of perfume and food, but George's stomach clenched instead of growling. He lifted his glass of wine as though to toast a passing colleague, but he drank to buy himself time. To look occupied, harmless, one more functionary in the safe, predictable ranks of Foreign Service officers.

No one could guess. He had been careful. Brilliant, even. The app he'd loaded onto Munro's phone was elegant, invisible, undetectable. When she spoke, he knew. When she wrote, he read. He wasn't stupid enough to keep the data on his work computer; no, he had a chain of digital dead drops, private accounts buried under layers of misdirection. He'd been paid well for the information he was able to get—Russians with their thick promises and thicker accents, the Chinese, so business-like, Neapolitan mobsters with flashy clothes and good haircuts and deadly smiles. Each payment more intoxicating than the last.

Soon it would be as if he were a trust fund baby too.

He had more than his miserable salary could ever have bought him—tailored shirts now, real wine instead of boxed, restaurants where the waiters knew his name. His colleagues pretended not to notice, and if they did...why not? It wasn't as though anyone openly said what George had known his whole professional life: that half of them were bankrolled by family money. Trust funds. Estates. Summers on Martha's Vineyard. He had nothing but his degree, his thinning hair, his drab government paycheck.

Until now.

. . .

"I wouldn't eat that, if I were you," Nick said just as the beautiful woman was about to pop the formless gray blob in her mouth.

"No?" She sighed and turned, keeping the blob in the small napkin. She looked up at him. "What do you suggest I do with it now? I mean I can't throw it on the floor. And I can't put it back on the tray."

Nick held out his hand and she placed the napkin in it. He sauntered over to the huge potted palm tree in the corner and leaned over as if observing something interesting in the broad avenue that ran along the bay. Nobody saw him deposit the napkin with the noxious blob in the soil. He also saw several other blobs. He wasn't the only one.

He sauntered back to the beautiful woman.

She smiled at him and ohmygod. No one should have a smile like that. It should be illegal. It was like the sun came out, on a sunny day in Italy.

Man, he'd spent too much time away from women.

Her smile widened. "That was well done. I didn't see a thing."

He bowed his head, leaned close to her and tried not to sniff like a dog. She smelled of something light and enticing. "I wasn't the only one with that thought," he said in a low voice.

Her eyes widened. "Others?"

"Hmm. You didn't taste it, but I did. I'm surprised this nice terrace isn't covered with that cr—stuff."

She sighed. "Poor Tobias."

"Tobias? The perpetrator has a name and it's Tobias? Here? In Naples?"

She made a little humming sound, lips curved. "The Consul General's grandnephew. Her sister persuaded her to let him intern here."

"That must have been some persuading. Naples must be full of excellent chefs. Where did Tobias study? The Culinary Institute of Dead Horse?"

"Close. The Herman Franklin Institute of Pastry in Cleveland."

Nick barely kept the wince off his face. "So I guess you know the Consul General fairly well if you know her staff choices." He held out his hand. "I'm Nick, by the way. Nikolai Garin."

She looked at his hand dubiously. He understood. He had big, visibly strong hands. He was a big guy, and he looked rough. There was no way for her to know he wouldn't crush her hand. Because he could, easily. Her hand was soft and delicate and looked extremely crushable, though he had no intention of crushing it. He would like to hold it, though.

He took her hand, held it for a moment, then let go, though he didn't want to. The way she looked at her still-intact hand was telling.

Nick stood, waiting for the second half of the introduction. He also wanted to hear her speak. She had a beautiful voice, clear and slightly husky. It also sounded weirdly familiar, though he knew for a fact he'd never met her before. He'd have remembered.

"Parker. Parker Donovan. Parker is a family name. I personally would have preferred Susan or Jane, but it is what it is. Do you live here, too?"

I wish, Nick thought. "No, my base is London. I'm here for a job."

Parker cocked her head. "Doing?"

He always had to be careful when talking about his job. Whatever he was doing, it was always secret, for security reasons. So he had to choose his words very carefully. Plus, her voice was distracting him, taking up a huge amount of his mental hard disk. "Consulting. I'm a consultant."

She smiled again and it nearly knocked him off his feet. "Consultant. I'll bet you're that big bad security guy Aunt Caroline hired to do a security overhaul of the Consulate. And I totally understand that you can't talk about it." She mimed zipping that beautiful mouth. "Nikolai Garin."

"Nick."

"Nick."

Busted. It wasn't that serious, though. He wasn't here under cover.

"So Caroline Munro, the Consul General, is your aunt?"

"Sort of. Honorary aunt. She's the stepmother of my best friend in boarding school. I've known her since I was ten, though Aunt Caroline was almost always away, rising through the State Department ranks. I've seen more of her, living here, than I ever did when I lived in Boston."

"You live here? Lucky woman."

She smiled again and Nick had to look away for a moment not to stare.

"Yes, it's quite enjoyable. Better weather than London."

"And better food."

"That, too. Except for what they serve at the Consulate."

He inclined his head. "Well, you know what I do. What do you do that requires you to live in this desolate, frozen outpost?"

She gave a small chuckle. "I'm a classicist."

He cocked his head and frowned a little.

She sighed. "My doctorate is in the classics. Greek and Latin. I love the ancient world. I wrote a book and made a documentary on the Etruscans."

A light went on in his head and he could feel his mouth fall open.

Ohmygod.

No wonder her voice was familiar.

"*The Smiling People*," he said, almost expecting her to deny it.

She smiled. "Yes, indeed. I'm flattered you've heard of it."

"Heard of it? I've watched it several times. Parker Donovan didn't click immediately. I think I assumed it was a man."

The Smiling People was one of the best documentaries Nick had ever seen. He saw it one evening in Afghanistan after a terrorist attack. He'd downloaded a bunch of stuff at the last minute before leaving and had downloaded some historical docs, while he was at it. *The Smiling People* was one of them and he had no idea what it was, just that any title with 'smile' in it was welcome.

He watched it on a day with no smiles. There'd been a mass suicide attack at an immunization station, and they managed to catch a couple of terrorists before they could off themselves. The men had been almost rabid, dying to die for no reason Nick could discern other than a visceral hatred of the 'West.' Interrogating them had been depressing and even degrading. That night he'd picked *The Smiling People* to watch because he thought he'd never smile again.

It had been charming and uplifting. A people who loved food and music, who lived in peace, never waging war in a thousand years. They lived on the border with Rome but never emulated Roman bellicosity.

The documentary compared the two civilizations and there was no contest. Except the Romans in the end conquered the Etruscans, and a peaceful, art-loving people were no more.

Parker had narrated it. That was why he recognized the voice.

"You weren't in the documentary. But it was yours."

She sighed. "I narrated it, yes, but it was pointless filming me, when there was so much Etruscan art to look at. Plus...a friend of mine did a documentary on dolphins and appeared on camera a lot and her life has not been worth living. People recognize her and either want to hug her or attack her. She's even gotten death threats. No thanks."

Nick frowned. "Death threats? Have you gotten any?"

She laughed. "Well, my policy of not appearing on camera paid off. I get spidery handwritten letters of enthusiastic thanks from ancient professors of Greek and Latin. The production company gets the emails. I don't even see them."

"Were there any threats in those emails?" Nick couldn't let the idea go. That this beautiful woman who'd created such a charming and uplifting documentary could be *threatened*. That went against everything he'd worked for all his life.

Those beautiful eyes looked to the side. "Maybe. But like I said, I don't see them."

Nick was eventually going to ask to see them. Because he was so intrigued by her, he was going to be seeing a lot of her. Unless she was engaged...

Fuck. He hoped not. But someone who looked like her? Who was smart and successful?

How to find out? Ask Caroline Munro in an unguarded moment? Maybe check her Facebook feed? Or maybe...

"Do you have a man in your life?"

Parker blinked slowly while Nick wanted to kick himself in the ass for asking the question so bluntly. He wanted to kick himself in the ass, but he also wanted the answer. Now.

She cocked her head and studied him for a minute. "That's not polite chitchat at a diplomatic reception."

Nick bit his back teeth. "No, it's not. It's intrusive and terrible manners and clumsy." *Though I want to know the answer.* "Professional deformation. I wasn't thinking of politeness, I was thinking as a security expert. I was thinking of what kind of system you have shielding you."

He hadn't been thinking that at all, but now that he'd said it, he did want to know. The security lobe in his head had been switched on.

Nowadays even librarians were getting death threats, and the threats were mostly noise, but not always.

"A system shielding me." Parker wrinkled her nose. "Well...technically, my agent? Though Everett isn't what you could really call a shield. However, he *is* good with contracts."

Nick had been leaning on the terrace parapet and slowly straightened. "I am going to sound intrusive and obnoxious. But I would really *really* like to take a look at some of those threatening emails. I have a program that can check email addresses for fictitious ones and can tell how long they have been in existence. If your producers kick up a fuss, say you've hired me. I'll give you a contract to sign. Objecting to *The Smiling People* is sick."

Parker looked at him, eyes like blue headlights. "You'd be surprised."

"No," he said firmly. He'd seen it all, twice. "I wouldn't."

"They object to me 'trashing the manly virtues of

Rome.' That was a direct quote. I have a 'radical feminist agenda' because I said women in Etruria were equal to men. People are crazy."

Yes, they were. And the crazy ones could do a vast amount of harm.

"You'll let me look at the threatening emails?"

"And letters."

"Through the postal system?"

"Yeah. Some had talcum powder inside the envelope."

The hairs on the back of Nick's neck stirred. To the uninitiated, talcum powder was indistinguishable from anthrax.

"I'd consider it a personal favor if you'd let me look into this. You don't know me but I'm sort of specialized in—" *shithead shenanigans.* "In dangerous situations."

"I know you are. Aunt Caroline said you were the best in the business and was really pleased you accepted the contract in person."

Because Italy had seemed like the perfect place to work in after a couple of years in unsavory places. And now he was really glad he'd accepted the contract.

"That means yes?"

"I guess it does. And thank you. My production company would probably cover your fee—"

Nick held his hand up, horrified. "No fee. No question of a fee. A favor for a friend."

Her lips curved. "Actually, we've just met."

"Not really. I've spent hours listening to your voice and ideas. As a matter of fact—" Nick looked away, over the gorgeous bay, at the light and life and beauty of the place. He hesitated. He wasn't used to sharing any but the most superficial of emotions, happy to keep his innermost thoughts completely to himself. But lately...well, lately he'd been feeling a little restless. A little empty. One could almost say a little lonely, only Nikolai Garin didn't do lonely.

Whatever it was, he found himself saying things that could never have come out of his mouth ten years ago when he'd been a hotshot commando, tough as nails. Invincible, uncrackable.

"A year ago, your documentary saved my sanity. My team and I had been hired by the World Health Organization to accompany and provide security for a team of doctors and nurses in Afghanistan. There'd been an outbreak of polio, and they were going to immunize the whole population of a region. We'd set up tents and they were immunizing several hundred people a day. There was this kid—Ahmed—who hung around. Skinny little guy who was completely fascinated by the procedure. By the tenth day he had an English vocabulary of about a hundred words and was really eager to help. We had a big security team because the immunization program was something the warlords hated. I'd just come back from patrol duty and was at one end of the encampment when I saw Ahmed. He was wearing a coat and looked like he'd put on twenty pounds."

She drew in a breath and covered her mouth.

Nick nodded sharply.

"Ahmed looked across at me and had the saddest look I've ever seen on a human face. Then he turned around and went into the immunization tent. I screamed and started running but I was too late. One half the encampment blew up. All ten doctors and fifteen nurses died. Together with two of my men and something like fifty locals. A forensic team came in and determined that Ahmed's bomb was remote controlled. They just...blew him up. They took a lively and affectionate and smart little boy and...blew him up. Together with their countrymen and twenty-five medical personnel working hard to keep their people safe from a deadly disease."

He drew in a deep breath. "That night I watched *The Smiling People* four times and it reminded me the world wasn't just pain and viciousness."

For a moment the sights and sounds of that awful day were superimposed on the amazing view right in front of him. That day still haunted his nights and had changed him in some fundamental way. He was still coming to grips with it.

He felt warmth on his arm and looked down. She'd put her hand on his arm. It wasn't in any way a come-on. It was a gesture of human connection. He put his hand over hers and held it there a moment.

Then reality rushed back in. He wasn't in Afghanistan, wounded and grieving and broken-hearted. He was in Naples, at the United States Consulate, on a freaking job.

"Sorry," he mumbled.

Parker shook her head, that shining fall of blue-black hair swishing across her shoulders.

And...the earth moved.

GEORGE WAS glad he had a chance to see the enemy, Nikolai Garin. George hadn't really gamed out what would happen if a security expert were called in. He'd expected to continue what he was doing because the Consulate staff were all lightweights, except for Caroline Munro. But she wasn't a technical expert.

Garin was.

George knew what Munro expected Garin to find—a leak, someone careless or compromised, some minor breach. But Garin would have to pass in review the entire Consulate. How could he possibly know how tech savvy George was? And yet George felt anxiety grip him.

It wasn't rational, that was the worst part. Objectively, he was safe. Perfectly safe. No one had ever caught the smallest trace of what he was doing. His app left nothing obvious. He had compartmentalized contacts, banked the bulk of the money safely in Aruba, never left a trail.

He knew intelligence. He knew how professionals worked. He wasn't some hacker selling compromising photos. He was a professional.

But still. Garin unnerved him.

Maybe he should cut back. Do one more job, maybe two, and then quit. Here in Naples, anyway. Do some investing. Step carefully. Start again in the next posting, and then the one after that. End up rich, with a laughable State Department pension.

And then Garin walked up to Parker Donovan. Just like that. Walked up to her, introduced himself and...she smiled at him.

What the hell?

George had always had to game it out when approaching Parker. Make it seem casual, not planned. Not that it ever made a difference, because Parker basically turned up her beautiful nose at him.

It made him deeply, bitterly resentful.

Parker smiled at something Garin said. She never smiled at him, never. She was always super polite, as she should be with her aunt's staff, but nothing more. She never gave him the warm smile she was giving Garin. Not once.

George forced his gaze away, lifted a glass to someone he saw across the terrace. A local businessman he cared nothing about.

Sipped his wine, which was good, but soured in his stomach.

Watched as Parker smiled again at the rich man who'd come to ruin his life.

And then the earth moved.

CHAPTER
Two

Parker didn't understand what happened. She'd put her hand on this giant's arm, this man she didn't know and yet she felt more of a connection with him than with anyone she'd recently met. How could she hope to comfort him, when she was nothing to him? But that story broke her heart. And his. She could tell.

He didn't look like a softie at all. In fact, he looked like he could chew glass. Very tall and immensely strong. There were a bunch of Army and Navy officers here on the Consulate terrace. Aunt Caroline made a point of always keeping good relations with military personnel wherever she was stationed and fully half the guests were military. Their invitations read *Dress Code: Summer Whites* and wherever they congregated in a group you had to shield your eyes from the glare. They were all tough men and women but Aunt Caroline's security consultant—

one Nikolai Garin—beat them at the toughness game. Effortlessly.

She'd been wondering how soon she could escape and go eat something somewhere that didn't taste as if it had been regurgitated by the seagulls wheeling overhead, when he'd suddenly appeared beside her.

Parker had had zero desire to flirt, but he hadn't flirted, or at least he hadn't said or done anything to make her uncomfortable. Of course, the fact that he was a fan was a *huge* argument in his favor.

And then he'd told her that story.

And then she'd put her hand on his arm, for comfort.

And then she found herself gripped in his arms, shaken off her feet. Or she would have been shaken off her feet if he hadn't pulled her to him in an iron clasp. The world moved, but Nikolai Garin didn't. He was as solid as a stone monument when everything around her shook.

The world had suddenly gone crazy, the ground moving literally beneath her feet. She held on to Nikolai like her life depended on it, burying her face in his chest, because he was the only stable thing in a tilting world.

One long breath, two, three, and the world stopped rocking. She held on for another moment, leaning against a warm, living wall. Then she pulled away, ashamed.

It had been an earthquake, not an apocalypse.

She leaned back against his arms, and he loosened his grip immediately. He held her shoulders and he carefully examined her. "You okay?"

"Y-yes. What—"

Parker looked around and finally focused on the world around her. Down along Via Acton, the boulevard which followed the bay, cars had driven off the road and drivers were honking. Almost all the parked cars had sirens wailing, mixing with the sounds in the distance of ambulances and police sirens. An earthquake with sound effects.

On the terrace, several waiters had dropped their trays to hang onto something, and the terrace was filled with glass shards and broken plates and food.

One woman—an Italian by her dress— was sobbing and someone—her husband perhaps—was trying to comfort her.

The American military officers were all tight-lipped, looking to someone gray-haired and with a chestful of fruit salad for instructions. She was giving orders while talking on a cellphone.

In the distance came the sound of an explosion.

"Gas line," Nikolai said.

Startled, Parker stepped completely out of his embrace. It had felt very natural to be near him during the earthquake, which was ridiculous. She had always been able to take care of herself and here the earth shook a little, and she cowered in a man's arms.

Big strong arms, but still.

"Epicenter Campi Flegrei," he said, consulting his phone. "5.5 on the Mercalli scale. What?"

She'd kept her expression neutral or tried to. But it seemed Nikolai Garin was unusually perceptive.

"Uhmm, nothing. It's just that our dig is near the Campi Flegrei, in Pozzuoli."

"A dig in a seismic zone, that's not good."

Parker sighed. "Can't do anything about it. That's where a Roman villa has been found. We'll be careful."

"If you're a classicist, not an archeologist, what are you doing on a dig?"

"Not digging, that's for sure. But I am gathering notes and taking photos."

Luckily, he didn't enquire what she was taking notes on. He looked around at the chaos on the terrace. Caroline Munro had arrived and was taking charge, but the reception was over.

Nikolai touched her elbow. "Looks like this whole thing is over. I have my car nearby. Can I give you a lift anywhere?"

She looked at him. Tall, broad, strong. She didn't know him, but her aunt did.

Still.

Never get in a car with a strange man had been drummed into her since she was a little girl. It was instinctive, though probably stupid in this case. He wouldn't do anything to her. Probably.

He didn't seem put out at her scrutiny. He just stood there, still and silent. She blew out a breath. "I came in a taxi and would appreciate a ride home, thank you. Sorry, I—"

"You were calculating whether it would be safe to get in a car with me," he said bluntly.

She bit her lips and said nothing.

"I understand completely, and I'd do the same in your shoes. I'd rather tear out my own throat than hurt you in any way, but you can't know that. I imagine the deciding factor was that your aunt knows me. And that, if nothing else, would stop me from hurting you because there would be blowback."

Parker hung her head. He put a finger under her chin and lifted her head. "I'm not saying this to shame you or anything. You're quite right to be careful. It's a bad world out there. You can't be too careful. But if you've decided, we should go before traffic becomes impossible. Shall we say goodbye to your aunt?"

Parker nodded her head.

Caroline Munro didn't have a protective attitude toward her. She hadn't had a protective attitude toward her own stepdaughter, but she'd want to know Parker's whereabouts in the aftermath of an earthquake.

"She's over in the corner," Nikolai said. He was taller than anyone on the terrace and was able to see her.

"No doubt directing the clean-up." She smiled. Aunt Caroline was super organized. Inside of an hour no one would know there had been anything amiss on the enormous terrace.

Nikolai put a huge hand on her back and directed them toward where he said her aunt was. But Parker still didn't see her. Caroline was fierce but small. Parker heard her voice before she saw her, ordering staff around.

Parker couldn't help herself, she looked up at the big man next to her and saw him smiling and smiled back.

"Yep, that's Aunt Caroline. I almost feel sorry for you, working for her."

The smile turned lazy. "Oh, I'll hold my own."

He was at least six foot four and probably weighed two thirty, all muscle. And he had that Master of the Universe vibe going. Aunt Caroline was a firecracker, but yeah, he'd hold his own.

There was a huge amount of confusion on the terrace, people disoriented, scared or annoyed. Plus a massive clean-up. Nikolai managed to guide them across the enormous terrace without slipping on anything or bumping into anyone. He had his hands on her shoulders, and no one bumped into her and given the chaos, that was a miracle. Everyone seemed to automatically get out of their way, then coalesce behind them.

It was a gift. People somehow scrambled out of their way, and they managed to avoid food messes, until they were right on the edge of a vortex of activity, with Aunt Caroline smack in the center.

"Giovanni, over here!" called Aunt Caroline and Parker saw her, pointing at a man in waiter uniform, then pointing to a corner of the terrace where a tray full of hors d'oeuvres had fallen. The area was slick with olive oil. "Clean that up with detergent after you sweep, so no one will slip on the oil. The last thing we need is a lawsuit."

The waiter nodded, heading for the corner with a huge broom and a big metal scoop.

Aunt Caroline looked up and saw them. She looked at Parker, at Nikolai, then back at Parker. Nikolai still had his hands on her shoulders and of course she saw that, too.

She walked up to them, nodding at Parker. "Hi, I guess you've got a ride home." She glanced sharply up at Nikolai, index finger out and pointing at him. "And you—you'll make sure she gets home safely," Aunt Caroline said. It wasn't a suggestion.

"Yes, ma'am," he answered, voice devoid of inflection. A simple statement. *I will get your honorary niece home safely*.

Aunt Caroline's shoulders dropped slightly, and Parker understood that, unexpectedly, for some reason, Aunt Caroline had been worried about her safety.

Aunt Caroline nodded. That was done, one thing ticked off her list. She had always been incredibly efficient. Aunt Caroline walked over to one of the officers, shook his hand and began speaking in earnest, having clearly forgotten all about them.

"Parker?" The big hands on her shoulders squeezed gently then dropped. "I think we should be going. We need to beat the traffic."

Parker smiled up at him. "Yeah, you're right."

He took her elbow, very lightly, and guided them off the terrace, down the elevator, past offices down to the monumental entrance. Every step of the way there had been Marines standing guard, super alert, as if they'd just lived through a terrorist attack and not an earthquake.

At the bottom of the stairs, Nikolai held his elbow at an

odd angle, and it took her a moment to realize he was offering his arm. It was curiously old-fashioned, but oddly reassuring, in a way. She slipped her hand in the crook of his elbow. The muscles of his arm were steel-hard and warm and solid. The earth had shaken, but he hadn't. They walked across a small park and down to the Bay. His legs were much longer than hers, but he kept pace with her.

Parker loved Naples. It had a very bad rep, sometimes justified. But it was chaotic more than crime-ridden. You quickly learned the areas to avoid, and you also learned to be incredibly vigilant.

As a single woman who wasn't ugly, Parker got a lot of unwanted attention. Neapolitan men somehow considered a single woman fair game, and she'd learned to walk fast, look straight ahead and never respond to catcalls, whistles, shouts. No looking around, enchanted by the surroundings. Pity, because Naples was so beautiful.

Like right now, the Bay gleaming sapphire and silver, the sky impossibly blue, Vesuvius a blue-gray giant on the horizon.

There was a controlled sort of bedlam in the streets. A lot of people had swarmed out of the buildings along the Bay. This hadn't been a bad earthquake. But earthquakes were weird, there were aftershocks, and if it *had* been a bad one, you wouldn't want to be in a building.

The streets were filled with people, some still scared, some delighted to be alive, some just happy to have had their work interrupted, like being let out of school early. It was so Neapolitan. Some theatrics, some people overreacting, some people wanting to party.

And everyone very loud.

A young man broke into a run, heading straight for them. He was waving at someone behind him and turned around just in time. He took one look at Nikolai and swerved.

Must be nice to be so intimidating that no one bugged you, no one ran into you, no one jostled you.

She wasn't intimidating at all. No one would mind running her down or brushing her shoulder. She often got unwanted comments and lascivious looks, whistles and shouts, someone trying to cop a feel. It was so tedious.

But not now. Now it was as if she were invisible, surrounded by a force field, and it was *great*. Nikolai's size and body language warned everyone off and she didn't think anyone would dare try to shout out a lewd comment or try to feel her up. Not with Nikolai by her side.

She was actually relaxed walking along the embankment in the hot sunshine. Parker loved Naples but it was a rough city for a single woman.

Another group of loud men was coming toward them, completely absorbed in themselves. They were raucous and not paying attention to where they were going. If she'd been alone, she'd have opted to walk around them or try to cross the street to avoid the tangle of men altogether.

Now...nope.

She sailed ahead on Nikolai's arm without a care in the

world, and sure enough, the group just split and flowed around them and regrouped behind them. Like magic.

She looked up at the blue, blue sky and the blue, blue sea, the sun reflecting off the tiny waves like pinpoint diamonds. To the left the city rose in a dramatic sweep of red and ochre and green buildings, set off by spectacular gardens. Such a delight to be able to enjoy it undisturbed.

"Must be nice being you," she sighed. Nikolai looked down, head cocked.

"Yeah?"

"Yeah. Those guys back there? They'd have run right into me and would have tried to cop a feel while they were at it. The other guy who was running toward us looking behind him? He'd have knocked me down, for sure." She studied him, tall and broad and strong. A force of nature. "No one's going to knock down Jack Reacher."

He gave a half smile.

"Not the first time someone's called you that," she guessed. He shook his head. "Must be nice. I have no desire to be a man, but if I did, I'd want to be you."

He looked down at her and his voice turned husky. "I am infinitely grateful that you are not a man."

It was definitely a suggestive comment, one of a million she'd received in her lifetime. She'd mastered the art of ignoring or deflecting and hated it. But somehow, his words didn't strike her as wrong, just sincere. He was happy she wasn't a man. And she was happy he wasn't a woman. There wasn't anything skeevy in his voice or demeanor. He didn't look smug or sly. Just stating a fact.

And then there was this curious reaction on her part. She didn't resent his comment. It...pleased her. The mildest flirtation possible, and it pleased her. She was happy to flirt with him.

He was attractive and she was attracted.

Naples was full of beautiful people, and since about fifty percent were male, there was something like a million good-looking men around, and she hadn't been attracted to one of them in the two years she'd been living here.

She was attracted to Nikolai Garin, which was strange because she knew nothing about him. He could be married for all she knew, though probably not. No ring—she'd checked. Not even a pale strip on his tanned hand. And though Aunt Caroline was no prude, she'd have somehow let Parker know if he was married.

He was a security expert. She had no idea what that entailed, but presumably it entailed a touch of paranoia and violence. Not things that ordinarily attracted her.

But he looked and talked like someone sane and even pleasant.

Parker was used to these types of thoughts. She'd come across almost every type of male unpleasantness that made for a bad companion, no matter how attractive the package.

She had the antenna of a hyena, that could smell carrion meat from a mile away. She could smell a man who was wired wrong.

Her system, which hadn't failed her yet, had given off no warning signals so far.

So...enjoy it. He would probably turn out to be terminally boring, or greedy, or something dire, and he'd be crossed off her mental list. But so far, he was definitely on it.

"Lotta complicated thoughts going on in that beautiful head of yours," he remarked. She looked up sharply.

He gently ran a finger down her face, the gesture over almost before she felt what he was doing. "You don't need to tell me what you're thinking. Not going to pry. But I would love to know."

Oh no. He was perceptive. This huge macho man, with muscles out to here, a man who worked in security, turned out to be sensitive to the thoughts and feelings of others.

Parker was used to keeping her thoughts to herself, but on her many dates, it wasn't hard. The guy was always more than eager to fill the void. More than willing to fill the airwaves with his job, always an important one, his car, cryptocurrencies, world events...

And she realized that this Nikolai hadn't once talked about his job, about how important he was, though she'd got it from Aunt Caroline that the Consulate had hired one of the best security guys in the world.

"I was thinking all over again how beautiful Naples is," she lied. She wasn't thinking that at all and she was well aware how beautiful the city was. "And now that I don't have to worry about people bumping into me, I can enjoy it more."

He smiled and tucked her hand more tightly into the

crook of his arm. "Don't worry about other people tripping you up."

Well, no. Not while she was by his side. He felt like a concrete pillar, and no one runs deliberately into a concrete pillar.

Such a beautiful place. It was possible to appreciate it now that she was all but invisible. The sparkling sea, with the ferries to the islands looking like tiny toy boats. Massive, centuries-old palm trees swayed gently in the breeze. Way farther down, you could barely see the huge cruise ships docked at Beverello Port, and farther still, on the horizon, across the Bay, Vesuvius.

This part of Naples was all baroque—huge sandstone palazzi dressed up as if for a Sunday parade.

And the light. Odes could be written about the light of Naples, a painter's dream. Living here, she often thought it a pity that she had no artistic talent at all. Probably better that way. She'd spend all her time on her balcony trying to capture the colors.

Some of the excitement of the earthquake had died down, and traffic was slowly getting back to its usual chaotic self.

"Naples was the largest city in Europe in the seventeenth century," she said. "Then it decayed quickly under misrule."

"A lot of places decay under misrule," Nick mused. "Seen it over and over again. And it's a tragedy, every single time."

"Like Rome. At the height of empire, it had over a

million and a half inhabitants. By the sixth century, it was in ruins with fewer than thirty thousand inhabitants. Some say the population fell to fifteen thousand. From a million and a half. Almost all the buildings were decayed."

Oops. She'd spoken without thinking and was probably boring him half to death. She looked up, expecting to find that usual expression of a suppressed yawn. "So sorry, I am probably boring you. I tend to get caught up in my enthusiasms."

His pale blue eyes widened. "God, don't apologize! This is fascinating. Like I said, I have seen so many places reduced to rubble. And a lot of atrocities where beautiful things were caught up in the madness and destroyed."

"The statues of the Buddha at Banyan," she murmured.

"Exactly." They were at the end of Piazza della Repubblica and Nick stopped. "My rental is in Piazza dell'Olio. Do we dare take our lives in our hands and cross?"

She was charmed at the idea that he hesitated crossing the busy avenue. He looked like a blond Superman. Cars would definitely bounce right off him. But they wouldn't bounce off her, and he seemed to have nominated himself as her protector, so they waited at the curb for traffic lights way up and down the avenue to stop cars and create a lull in the traffic.

Finally, there were no cars coming in either direction. It wouldn't last. She could hear cars revving their engines. Neapolitans didn't like traffic lights, particularly when they were red.

They looked at each other and grinned.

"Go!" he said and they went.

She didn't know how he did it. His legs were much longer than hers, but he kept exact pace with her, only she'd somehow been kicked into a faster gear. In an instant they were across the street, just in time. Cars started whizzing past them.

Nick withdrew his arm from around her waist, and she realized he had almost carried her across without her noticing. It had been a little like flying.

And...plastered to that super strong body, *she'd* felt invincible. As if the cars would bounce off *her*. It was a delicious feeling.

And...she'd felt heat. Not just from his body but from hers. She'd been so close she could feel all those muscles, which weren't just for show. They were warm and steely and felt amazing.

Her entire body had been shocked by the contact, and even now, on the other side of the street, she could still feel him.

It had been incredible. She laughed.

Nick smiled down at her. "What's funny?"

"Well, not funny, actually. It's just that crossing streets in Naples is like entering the gladiator ring. You never know if you'll make it out alive. You made me feel invincible. Incredible."

His smile broadened. "Want to go again? We could cross back over and come back. Would you like that?"

Hmm. A chance to be plastered up against that strong body again. Oh man...

But...she was an adult and had to be a grownup about it.

"Tempting as that sounds, I think we should get to your car."

"Well, we're here." They had reached one of the thousands of tiny piazzas that served as paid parking spots.

She blinked. "We are?"

He knocked on the fender of a big black beast, more a tank than a car. "Yep. Here she is."

"You are driving around Naples in *that?*"

"I was assured it is what the mafiosi drive and no one would dare steal it." He shrugged. "It's a rental anyway."

He opened the passenger side door, and she looked in dismay at the step. It was a long way up and she was wearing a tight skirt. Sighing, she grasped the side of the door and was preparing to haul herself up when two strong hands grasped her waist and she was lifted up onto the seat like magic.

"Hey." She turned to look at him. He looked serious. "Sorry to manhandle you like that, but these SUVs are built really high off the ground. And since I'm apologizing, I'll also apologize for grabbing you when we crossed the street."

He was standing in the open doorway, one hand on either side of the door. He was frowning slightly.

Parker had been manhandled a lot in her life. Guys

often used the flimsiest excuse to cop a feel and no one, not once, had ever apologized. Or look dismayed.

But not Nick. He actually looked...a little worried, so odd on that tough face. She smiled at him. "Well, considering that all the drivers in the city have been driven crazy by the earthquake and we took our lives in our hands crossing Via Caracciolo, I'm actually grateful I survived the experience. And—" she fingered her linen skirt. "This is a designer outfit and wouldn't have survived me scrabbling to get up and onto this seat, so I have two things to thank you for. Thank you. Twice."

That tough face cleared. "My pleasure." He got into the driver's seat and turned on the engine. "So what's the address?"

"Via Verdi 327. It's halfway up the Vomero. That's the—"

"The hill right in front of us, yes." He tapped in the address on the navigator and took off.

Parker sat back, not wanting to disturb him. Every once in a while, the traffic in Naples was touched by Satan and this was one of those days. Instead of a straight progression, traffic was in Brownian motion, more circular than linear. Full of bottlenecks and traps. The car was sound-insulated, but still the sound of a thousand honking horns trickled in.

Nightmare traffic and it had always scared her. Most days, traffic was a little chaotic, but if you went slow and gave others the right of way, you could eventually make your way home in relative safety.

Today was not one of those days.

It had her in a sweat, and she was a passenger.

Nick, however, didn't seem to be affected at all. He drove as if they were on a deserted country lane. She was sure he'd never been in her part of town, which was residential, with no monuments or museums, and yet he drove straight there as if he'd done it a hundred times before, only checking a few times the GPS screen.

A few blocks from home, she realized she could talk to him without distracting him and causing an accident. The traffic was one endless snarl, as if the minor earthquake had messed with people's heads. "Amazing how you seem unfazed by the traffic. Today is the worst I've ever seen it."

He turned his head to smile at her, then returned his attention to the road where someone ran a red light, nearly killing a family of five.

"I've driven under fire, this is nothing."

Oh. Well, yes. Bad as the traffic was, no one was actually shooting at them.

"What do you drive?" he asked.

Hmmm. This was where he would become scathing. "I drive a Smartcar."

She braced, because she'd heard it all before. She could afford any car she wanted, and she chose *that*? It was barely a car, might as well shop in the toy department, what was it good for?

"Good choice," he said, and she peered at him to see if he was being sarcastic.

But no. He seemed perfectly serious. "What?"

"City like Naples, a Smartcar is a really good choice. It's very maneuverable, easy to park, fabulous mileage."

Well, that was interesting. "If you think it's such a good choice, what are you doing with this massive monster?"

He reached out and patted the dash, the way a cowboy pets his favorite horse. "Never know when I might need to go out of town and need some power. We're here."

He swerved suddenly and parked right in front of her apartment building, in a tight space she couldn't have managed in one maneuver not even with her tiny Smartcar. She'd been so fascinated by him that she hadn't even noticed they were in her neighborhood.

Parker reached for the door opener, but he put a hand on her arm, gently, and only for a moment. She stopped.

"I know we've only just met, but I'm hoping your honorary aunt can vouch for my morals and respectability. I have a reservation tonight at Il Terrazzone. I'd be honored if you would join me for dinner."

Parker turned and looked at him, not hiding what she was doing. He just sat there, still, understanding she wanted to take the measure of him.

It was true. He was doing business with Aunt Caroline, who was smart, no-nonsense, and would never hire a man with a reputation of shadiness or dishonesty and would definitely have hired the most competent person she could.

But being good at your job was no guarantee that he

would be a good dinner companion. The worst date she'd ever been on had been with a Vice President of one of the ten biggest banks in the world. He'd been obnoxious, touching her all through dinner, bragging about how rich he was, and had used a little violence when kissing her outside the restaurant. She'd had to push him and run around the corner to catch a taxi and her last glimpse of him had been through the rear window as he lifted a fist at her, handsome face twisted with rage.

So professional success and wealth meant nothing. You could be rich and successful and still be a jerk.

And yet...

There had been no bad behavior on his part. He'd been a perfect gentleman, hadn't made her feel uncomfortable once. Had got her across the street in Neapolitan traffic on a bad day. That earned him serious points.

"Il Terrazzone is one of the nicest restaurants in Naples," she said.

"So I've heard. I was resigned to one of those really nice meals on my own. If I had your company, it would make it memorable."

Well, put like that... "Yes. I'd like that."

He grinned, a sudden blossoming of pleasure on his face that made him look ten years younger.

How old was he? He had such an air of command and was clearly at the top of his profession. He had lines on his face, which she now saw were probably more from sun and wind than age. He definitely did not look like the moisturizing type.

Not only that. To be called by the US Consulate was a big deal, and only well-known professionals were called. She'd assumed he was in his forties but now, with that grin, light blue eyes gleaming, she saw he could be closer to her in age. Mid-thirties maybe.

"How old are you?" she blurted out and immediately regretted it. But it was out there.

"Thirty-eight," he said, without blinking.

She was thirty-two. So. Not *that* big of an age gap.

"Now that we've got that out of the way." Nick kept his hands on the wheel, just turning his head to look at her. "My reservation is at eight. Should I pick you up at seven-thirty?"

"You do realize that is an insanely early hour for dinner in Naples?"

He nodded. "I got that from the hotel concierge, who looked appalled. However, I'm told that the terrace is magnificent with a great view over the Bay. We could have drinks on the terrace until it's a reasonable hour for dinner in Naples."

"We could," she agreed. These days she rarely accepted a dinner date from someone she'd just met. But... her dinner tonight was going to be a slice of mozzarella with cherry tomatoes, a huge peach and half a glass of a dry white wine. Then scrolling to find something on Netflix to watch.

Dinner with Nikolai Garin at Il Terrazzone sounded much better. If it turned out that he was a jerk after all, at least she'd have had a nice meal in a beautiful setting.

His face was turned to hers and she scrutinized him. He didn't look like a jerk, and he was amazingly attractive without being handsome. And he was built. When he'd held her close to his side to cross that dangerous street, he'd felt like warm steel.

If you'd asked her whether she was susceptible to beefcake, Parker would definitely have said no. And yet, here she was. "I'd like that."

He smiled and by the lines in his face, she could tell he didn't smile often.

"Great. I'll walk you to your door."

She smiled back. "The door's right there." She pointed out the window. "Nothing bad is going to happen to me in the five steps from the vehicle to the door."

But she was talking to empty air because he'd rounded the SUV and was opening her door for her. And, like before, he simply lifted her out and down, releasing her immediately as soon as her feet touched the ground.

He looked around. Her street was quiet, with leafy linden trees. So high up the Vomero they could barely hear the chaos down on the bay. The buildings were all made of stone and at least a hundred years old. "Nice area."

"It is. I was lucky." He was looking at her intently and she couldn't take her eyes off his face. It felt like they were frozen, gazing at each other, until a car went by, the driver honking impatiently at a pedestrian jaywalking. "Though there are impatient drivers up here, too."

Nick nodded. "I'll wait until you're inside the door."

She checked his face, to see if he was joking, but he

was dead serious. If no one was lying in wait in the few steps from the vehicle to the door, it was a sure bet nothing bad could happen on her doorstep. Yet he stood there, stolid, unsmiling, waiting for her to enter her building. To make sure it was done safely. She realized what it meant to be an expert in security. It meant you dealt in situations that were unsecure, unsafe. And he'd probably been in plenty of those places.

She kept her housekeys in an outside pocket of her bag. In a moment, her big heavy front door was open, and she stopped, one foot in, one foot out, and looked back.

Oh God, he was such a magnet for the eyes. Tall, broad, yet lean and athletic, he had such a physical presence. Like he had a gravity of his own, and he was pulling her toward him. She grasped the door lintel to keep from falling toward him.

Again, they gazed at each other without moving.

He definitely messed with her head, and she wasn't entirely sure if she liked it.

"Well, I'll um..." Parker gestured toward the elegant, dark lobby behind her.

"Yeah. I'll wait for the door to close behind you."

In case a bear was in wait in the lobby.

"Okay. See you later."

She pulled the heavy door closed and it felt like she'd been cut off from a source of intense energy.

She climbed the stairs to her apartment slowly, because her knees felt weak.

This wasn't good. Not at all.

Still.

She was going to wear her brand-new turquoise summer dress.

N ick nearly swallowed his tongue when Parker answered the door. He'd spent an hour walking the waterfront, trying to calm himself down, before going back to his hotel and taking a shower. A cold one.

Until she opened her apartment door, he'd managed to convince himself that he'd had a brain melt, reacting to her so strongly.

He was tired, he'd been working nonstop without a break for almost two years. He'd been working in failed states mostly. Places where women were kept under wraps quite literally. They were poor creatures who scuttled from home to market and back. His professional dealings had been with men who were brutal, understood only the crudest of power.

Nick himself was immune to the men, had a force field around him that protected him. He was a Westerner, was rich, was there usually upon their government's request, and he himself was strong, was a really good shot, and had been trained in martial arts. No one touched him, though they would have liked to.

Not so for the women. They were screamed at, caned, beaten with sticks and stones. The same for the kids and dogs. He knew he couldn't intervene, but it sickened him. His time there had felt endless and was certainly sexless. Any woman he had sex with would be killed. Somehow, in the back of his mind, the other sex had become this beaten down group, dressed in sacks, heads and faces covered, objects of pity, certainly not lust.

Parker—whoa. Not a figure of pity, no way. So beautiful you had to work not to stare at her. And so bright, like a shining star. And the author of *The Smiling People!* That book and that documentary had kept him company in many a long, lonely night in terrible places, reminding him that humans could be civilized, too.

But...maybe he'd been blown away and she wasn't as enticing as he remembered?

That was always a possibility. After so long in unsavory places, maybe he had like the bends and had blown her up to something she wasn't in his head.

Nope. When she answered the door, he nearly sighed. Somehow, she was even more beautiful than he remembered.

"Hi," she said, and he made some kind of sound with his mouth. "Sorry I'm running a little late. I'm never late, but I had a zoom call with my publisher, and it dragged on."

She was chatty and friendly, but all of a sudden, she stopped, frowning. "What? What's wrong? Do I have lipstick on my teeth, or something?"

"Huh?" he said. And then realized he had stopped, frozen just inside the door, and was staring at her.

Creeps stared at women. It was a tool of intimidation but also stalkerish. That's not what this was. It's just that he was frozen. She was so fucking beautiful she ate up his entire hard disk.

Maybe it was wrong, him meeting her just back from the badlands. He wasn't used to beautiful, smart women. It bunged up his brain and tangled his tongue.

"Nick?" She was frowning and had taken a step back.

That shocked him out of his paralysis. He was making her afraid of him. Goddamn, that was the last thing he wanted.

Get your head out of your ass, stat! he told himself sternly.

"Sorry," he said, shaking his head. "Had a little fugue state there. About work."

The little lie worked. Parker relaxed. "Had a few myself. Would you like a drink while you wait? I still need a few minutes."

A few minutes? He'd wait months, years for her. A few minutes was nothing.

Nick smiled at her. "No, I'm fine. I'll just sit down and wait. Done a lot of that in my career. A lot of soldiering is just waiting around. I've got waiting around down to a fine art." Hours lying immobile in a hide, pissing in a bottle.

Hours traveling in a fiercely uncomfortable C-130, strapped to the bulkhead, pissing in a bottle. Hours on surveillance, pissing in a bottle.

This—this on the other hand, was sheer heaven. He looked around. Parker's apartment was a delight, like the inside of a music box. She had antique furniture, nothing modern. But not trophy antique furniture— they looked like things that had been used generation after generation. Antique rugs and what looked like real art on the walls. The total effect was charming and soothing. To add to the sensory overload, classical music was playing. He was a musical barbarian and had no idea what it was—there were flutes and a harp and a piano—but it was better than a beta blocker to slow down the heart.

The last rays of the sun slanted in from the French doors open to a wrought iron balcony, filling the room with golden light, making everything shine.

Just sitting there made him feel better. And on top of that, the most beautiful woman he'd ever seen was in the other room, getting ready to go out to dinner with him.

His last job had been in one of the 'Stans, a six-month long contract on behalf of the DOD to get a local warlord to sign a treaty respecting human rights. The warlord had no intention of respecting the treaty, and even getting him to sign had been a crash course in human psychopathology, as if Nick needed that. It had involved going hunting with the psychopath, clubbing with the psychopath, and eating with the psychopath who had the table manners of a feral boar. He'd had to watch him behave like a monster, smiling all the while, trying to inculcate some values of decency in a man who had none. And in the evening, he'd go back to his dusty, uncomfortable hotel, which was the best in the city, and take a half-hour shower trying to scrub Fuckhead Psycho off his skin.

His company had made eight million dollars, and the fuckhead had signed, which calmed things down around his borders and maybe some lives would be saved. But he'd counted the minutes before he could leave and heaved a sigh of relief as his company plane took off.

Originally, once his last contract finished, he'd just wanted to go home. But home wasn't really home, it was just a place. He'd chosen London as his home base because it was in a convenient time zone, but what was waiting for him was a deluxe flat in the center of the city that was half empty, felt empty, even smelled empty, and was more alienating than a hotel room.

And it had rained in Psycholand for weeks. The streets had instantly become pools of mud, since the company that paved the streets was owned by the President-For-Life's nephew and he was a cokehead who didn't have the faintest clue about road maintenance.

Nick needed someplace warm and sunny and welcoming. His next job was scheduled in Naples in four days, so he decided to give himself a few days off and flew directly to Naples.

Man, was he glad he did.

Parker came out of her bedroom, and he stood. Oh God. How could any woman be so beautiful? It was like she shimmered when she walked. She had on an elegant summer dress the exact color of her eyes.

She blinked at him. "Is something wrong? Are we late?"

"No." Nick almost took a step back when she walked up to him. Fuck, he never took steps back no matter what. "Why?"

She touched his arm, and Nick felt a little electric shock. "You stood up so abruptly. Why did you—oh!" Those cobalt-blue eyes widened. "You stood up because I walked into the room? Not often you see that. Someone brought you up right."

He had an answer for that.

"My father is very old school, instilled manners in me and chided me if I forgot them, particularly in the presence of ladies." He grinned. "My mom, on the other hand, is brutal and would smack me if she didn't like my behavior. You learn quickly. I didn't want to disappoint my father, and I was terrified of my mother."

She studied his face. "No, you aren't. You aren't terrified of your mother."

No, he wasn't. He shrugged. "Busted. The truth is, my mom is a nice lady who is a stickler for manners. She was appalled when I joined the military. To her, the military is made up of barbarians." Appalled was a weak word. Both his parents did everything but tie him up so he wouldn't enlist, but he'd been unstoppable. They didn't talk to him for a month.

Her head tilted. "What did they want you to do?"

"I think my mom was hoping I'd teach. History maybe, because she is a history buff. My father was hoping for the sciences because I was decent at math."

She studied him carefully, close scrutiny by those eyes that were shards of sky. It wasn't a hardship. He let her look all she pleased. She looked him carefully up and down. Finally, she gave a half smile. "I've been among historians all my adult life and I think I can safely say that you look nothing like an historian."

He raised his eyebrows. "That's a good thing?"

The smile broadened. "A very good thing." She glanced out the window where the sun was low in the sky, flooding the Bay with golden light. "Maybe we should be going?"

The light still flooded the apartment too, picking out glints in silver frames, an alabaster vase full of flowers, the brass pull handles on a chest of drawers. It turned the room golden. He smiled.

"Something funny?" Parker tilted her head.

He looked down at her, happy about everything. Happy about where he was, happy that he was with Parker in this beautiful room. Happy that they were going to go out for what would undoubtedly be a spectacular meal and that no one would shoot at them on the way. Happy that she was good company. And decided to say the truth. Why the fuck not? Nick never ever revealed what he was thinking or feeling, certainly not to a woman he'd just met. But hell, it just spilled out anyway.

"Do you know where I was exactly a year ago today?"

She shook her head.

"I was in a shithole country which shall be nameless, where you take your life in your hands walking down a street after the sun has gone down. I was brokering a peace between two warlords who were brothers and who hated each other. Their war was killing a lot of innocent people, and we managed to come to a conclusion where they could still hate each other's guts but share in lording it over a country reduced to ashes by their war.

"I was staying in the nicest hotel in town, and it smelled of piss and boiled goat meat, with an overlay of whiskey and cheap perfume. The two men were both cruel and untrustworthy, borderline crazy, and I had to shower after spending any time with either of them. And now look at me." He waved his hand around the charming living room, glistening with light. "In a lovely apartment that smells of lavender, about to go to a famous restaurant with a beautiful woman. My fortunes have definitely improved."

Her expression didn't change at hearing herself called a beautiful woman. Nick had told a number of women that they were beautiful, though none of them could touch Parker. They all changed expression at the words, either turning coy or batting away the compliment in a fit of false modesty.

Parker did nothing. But then she'd probably been told she was beautiful all her life. She'd probably been a beautiful child and beautiful teenager, too. It sure hadn't sidetracked her. She'd built an amazing career that had nothing to do with her looks, and everything to do with her smarts. And to have produced that documentary, she had business smarts too.

"So being here is an upgrade?"

"Definitely an upgrade. You about ready? If not, I can wait."

Parker reached behind her for her purse and put on a gauzy summer jacket. "I'm ready. And hungry. Didn't have any lunch and the food at the Consulate reception, as you know, wasn't great."

Nick put a hand to the small of her back, sorry that he was touching gauzy silk and not silky skin. He replayed what she'd just said and frowned. "How come you didn't have lunch?" She was very slender and shouldn't be skipping meals.

"I was finalizing a chapter I sent to my agent and didn't have time for lunch, and anyway, I thought there'd be food at the Consulate reception. But, as we know, that didn't work out too well." She tilted her head, studying him. "If I'd had a mother, you would sound just like her. Worrying about what I had for lunch."

"You didn't have a mother?" He blinked, momentarily sidetracked. "You were hatched?"

"No." She smiled. "But my mother died giving birth to me. I have no memory of her."

"Wow. I'm sorry." Nick tried to imagine his family without his strong-willed mother and failed. "Growing up without a mom is tough. Your father never remarried?"

Her face closed up, just froze, as if it were a fist that tightened. "No, he never remarried. I'm ready."

Nick had been around a few blocks and recognized a closed door when he saw one. "Great." He opened her door. "Off we go. We might even be on time which I understand would be a first in Naples."

CHAPTER
Four

They were shown to an amazing table at the edge of the huge terrace overlooking the Bay. The best spot in the house. Parker thought she'd seen Nick discreetly slip the maître-d' some money but she wasn't sure. Didn't even want to know. Knowing might spoil some of the magic of the evening.

It was definitely magical.

The sun had just set behind Vesuvius, the clouds tinged with gold, setting the city aglow. Lights were turning on all over the city and the ornate streetlamps along the bay switched on.

Nick pulled out her chair, choosing for her the one that faced the bay, and then sat down to her right, which gave him a view over the entire terrace. He always seemed preternaturally aware of everything, whether walking or driving.

Professional paranoia, she assumed.

Parker sighed as she took in the magnificent view, reputedly the best in the city. She'd never been to Il Terrazzone, not because she couldn't afford it—though apparently it was wicked expensive—but because she didn't have anyone to go with.

She did, now.

She sighed again in happiness. Looked around, smiling. "This is gorgeous."

His eyes had never left her face. "Yes, absolutely gorgeous."

His meaning was very clear, but somehow non-skeevy. How did he manage that? He smiled, looked behind her. "The waiter is coming up. You said you wanted a drink first?"

She nodded. "Yes, please."

The idea was enticing. Aperitivo on the terrace, enjoying the sunset, then a spectacular dinner. No hurry, no hurry at all. She was very much in a no-hurry mood.

"Then that's what we'll do."

A waiter dressed like the butler to a prince glided up. Parker turned to Nick. "What would you like? Wine? A Negroni? A cocktail? A spritz?"

He continued watching her. "Whatever you have is fine with me."

She frowned. "I was going to order a glass of rosé, which you might find boring."

"Don't worry." Nick gave a slow smile. "I am so far from being bored it's insane. A glass of rosé sounds great. You order the vintage."

She had a brief consultation with the waiter, and they decided on a Sicilian rosé she was familiar with. "I hope that's okay with you." She smiled at Nick. "It's a really good wine. Donnafugata from Sicily, an estate wine. But, again, if you'd rather have a brandy or a whiskey—"

He picked up her hand and held it. His hand was huge, warm, heavily calloused, and it felt like she plugged into something big, electric. He nodded at the terrace and the view over the Bay. "Please. This is all so wonderful. I'm absolutely certain you chose a fabulous wine and that I'll enjoy the hell out of it."

"I hope so."

Nick left her hand and lifted his big one to run his thumb between her eyebrows. "There are a lot of things you should frown over. It's a harsh world. But me not liking a wine you've chosen is not one of them. I can tell you, right here and right now, that this is the best situation I've been in, in years. A beautiful view, in a beautiful city, sitting with a beautiful and fascinating woman...couldn't ask for more."

It was the second time he'd called her beautiful. Without making it a big deal. Because it really wasn't. It was genetics. Her mother had been a beauty, at least in the photos Parker had of her. And her father, miserable human being that he was, was very handsome. Both had fine features she'd inherited. It didn't have much to do with her. What did have to do with her was her work—her books and the documentary and Nick had been very flattering and gratifying about those.

She enjoyed his compliments about the documentary more than she enjoyed his compliments on her looks. Though—those were nice, too.

"*Signori.*" The waiter, holding a bottle of Donnafugata. He deftly uncorked the bottle and held it up.

Nick waved a long finger at her, leaving it up to her to taste it and approve it. Well, at least she knew it was an excellent wine.

The waiter poured a finger, and she sipped. It tasted of sunshine, fruit and happiness. She nodded.

The waiter poured them both generous measures. Nick indicated that he should leave the bottle, and the waiter put it in a bucket stand with ice.

"Really good stuff," Nick said after sipping. "Thanks. I wouldn't have known to order it. The advantages of being with a local. I might have missed out on this."

"Maybe not." Parker smiled. "The waiter might have suggested this wine with the meal. It's one of the pricier ones."

Nick shrugged, as if that didn't mean anything to him. Maybe it didn't.

Nick took another sip, put it down. She liked that he wasn't gulping it. It was definitely a wine to savor.

He cocked his head. "You said you were talking to your publisher. Are you writing another book?"

Oh man. The way to her heart. "Yes. Yes, I am."

"Can I know what it's about? The Etruscans again? Another aspect? I'll buy it the instant it's out."

"You don't have to do that. I'll gladly give you a signed copy."

His light blue eyes glowed. "Oh, man. I'd love that. So, what will it be about?"

She waited, looked at him. He didn't seem to mind the scrutiny. What did she know about him? Well, that her Aunt Caroline, who was no one's fool, had chosen him to advise the Consulate in a serious manner. He didn't seem to be wanting for money, so he probably wouldn't try to sell the idea.

More than all that, though, the impression he gave was that of a serious man. Not a light weight. Not someone who tried to charm his way through life. His entire body language was that of a fully grown man, serious and sober and reliable, unlike so many men who were adults in age but not behavior.

A man's man. The real deal. She had to curl her hands to keep from touching him. He exerted some kind of force of gravity on her, as if he were a moon. It was hard to keep from leaning into him. Was she being swayed by that?

Whatever. She was going to tell him what her next book was about, whether that was wise or not. And even though her publisher had begged her not to.

"My—my publisher has asked me not to talk about the book. To make sure it has an impact upon publication that hasn't been spoiled. I'll have to ask for your discretion."

He didn't look offended. "Please don't worry about that. I spent most of my military career on classified missions that will remain secret till the end of time. My companies—I am a part-owner of Go Solutions and am a part-owner of Black Inc.—are known for being utterly reliable. So, betraying a confidence—particularly one that might harm you? Not going to happen, ever."

Wow. Part-owner of Black Inc., which was the premier security company in the world. He wouldn't be tempted by money. Certainly no one could buy him.

And...and she wanted to tell him. There hadn't been anyone to talk to about it. Aunt Caroline was friendly, but to her, the posting to Naples was a geopolitical consideration. Naples was an important city in the Mediterranean, home to a major naval installation of the Sixth Fleet. Aunt Caroline had no interest whatsoever in the past, let alone the remote past.

The only person she'd communicated with at her publishing house was her editor, who was enthusiastic, but looked and acted as if she were twelve. Parker didn't know how great a grasp Emily had on history. For her, history started with Obama, when she was eight.

So Parker hadn't been able to talk it over with anyone. And here was this huge man, who looked like he ate nails for breakfast, but had watched *The Smiling People* again and again. Who seemed so at ease in the world. Why not?

"Okay." Parker leaned forward a little and so did he. His shoulders were so broad they blocked her view. But more than that, he exerted a sort of force field around him that pulled her toward him. She had to mentally nail herself to her seat not to tip over into his lap.

Sigh.

It was sort of a pity he was so immensely attractive, so utterly...male. And was so very unobnoxious. She was drowning in her own hormones.

But it also felt right. This beautiful evening, on the gorgeous terrace of a restaurant known for its exquisite food, in a city renowned for its beauty, with an interesting and fascinating man, seemed like the right setting to discuss her project, a project of the heart.

One thing she knew—he would listen carefully and not make fun of her obsessions. Most men she dated would listen to her for about five minutes before launching into long talks about themselves and would find some way to dismiss her passions as unimportant.

Nick was totally focused on her.

She folded her hands in front of her and prepared to essentially make a pitch for her idea, the first time since she pitched it to her agent and her baby editor. Maybe this was a chance to see if it flew with the general public.

"You know those billionaires buying mansions they turn into fortresses in places like New Zealand, preparing for the end of the world?"

His mouth quirked. "I was security consultant for three of them. Two tech bros and a hedge fund owner. The two tech bros basically wanted to make sure their game rooms would work forever, and the hedge fund owner was terrified of what would happen when his money no longer counted in a world brought back to the Dark Ages. He was seriously contemplating fitting his security staff with permanent shock collars."

Parker's eyes widened. "Wow. People go a little crazy when their status is threatened, that's true. Well, all the books say that our modern world could disappear in a second. Technology—whoosh, gone."

Nick's head dipped. "Yeah. It could all go south in an instant. A Carrington Event that takes out the electrical grid, for example. It's estimated that it would take twenty years to get the grid back up and running and, in the meantime, humankind would go feral. Or even a limited nuclear war. Or a new virus a hundred times worse than COVID. Or AI becomes Skynet. Lots of different ways to go."

"That's right. So, here's the thing. Civilization has already been destroyed once—the fall of the Roman Empire. It wasn't fast, it was slow, but for those who had eyes to see, it was inevitable. The Roman Republic was very stable—politically and economically. It was self-sufficient in food and was defended by a citizen army. Then Rome expanded and became an Empire, with a professional army. But from the Julians—Caesar and his descendants—on, as the Empire was established and started growing, Rome became restless, corrupt. The classes solidified and there was very little movement between them, whereas during the Republic many peasants ascended to what we would call the middle class. That almost stopped completely during the Empire. The bureaucracy became corrupt, inefficient. General health deteriorated. There are estimates that the average life expectancy during the Republic was about fifty-two, which dropped to forty-five during the Empire. And fell to about thirty-five during the Dark Ages. I hope I'm not boring you."

He covered her hand again and the warmth spread from her hand up her arm. "I am the furthest thing from bored, trust me."

He looked serious as he said it. Okay. Better than okay, actually. Parker was used to male interest, but it was rarely in what she had to say. She was used to men getting a glazed look in their eyes when she talked about classical history. They would fake interest for a few minutes, their entire attention span, then change the subject. But not Nick. His pale blue eyes were fixed on her, and he was unmistakably engaged in what she was saying.

"From the time of Claudius onward, the fall of Rome was inevitable, it just took another three hundred years. But in the meantime, if you could see the signs, you knew the end was coming. The empire was so large it was almost impossible to manage, and the barbarians along the border were becoming more and more aggressive. It was clear the center couldn't hold. I've combed the literature of the time, and of course nothing could be said in any official documents. Rome was eternal and you would be punished if you said anything to the contrary. But I've read a lot of private correspondence that tells me the idea of the Fall of Rome was in the air. So, increasingly, members of the dwindling middle class and of the aristocracy would buy estates far from Rome, often in the warm and fertile lands of the south of Italy and establish a bolt hole in case Rome fell. Often, they would move their entire household, which sometimes comprised hundreds of people. There was a very quiet scramble to get out of Rome, far from its reach, as a survival mechanism. The earliest preppers if you will. It's estimated fifty thousand aristocrats fled Rome during Caligula's reign alone. They could feel the craziness in the air. The working title of my book is *Apocalypse Then.*"

Nick's eyes widened. "That's—that's pure genius," he breathed. "And fascinating. You must write it, and I want the first signed copy. Hot off the press."

"Done." She smiled.

"*Signori.*"

They both looked up in surprise. The tuxedoed waiter again. "Would you like to look at the menu?"

He laid on the table two big, printed menus, in script font, with only a few dishes per course, a sure sign of a good restaurant. He'd interrupted them, but Parker didn't mind. All of a sudden, she had a huge appetite. It wasn't just skipping lunch. She often skipped meals. No, her appetite somehow was tied to the giant man sitting next to her, paying careful attention to what she said. She felt open. And warm. What you felt during sex, or so she'd read. Wide open, full of heat. They weren't in bed, so the restaurant equivalent of sex was a roaring appetite, antici-pating pleasure.

Parker opened a menu, sliding the other one over to Nick. He slid it right back to her.

"You order for me. Things you'd like to eat as well, and we'll share. That okay with you?"

She smiled. "More than okay. Everything looks great and it's going to be hard to choose."

"Order everything you'd like to taste," Nick commanded.

"Whoa. That could be a lot of food. Do you eat fish?" Parker looked up from the fish-heavy menu.

"I eat everything except goat. I've eaten nothing but goat for the past couple of years and I'm sick of it."

She ran her eye down the menu. "Not a mention of goat. You're going to have a goat-free meal, guaranteed."

He sat back, grinning. "Then I'm good. Order a bunch of stuff. I want to sample everything."

Oh. He basically wanted a sampler menu, but the restaurant didn't offer one. She'd have to order full plates. "You'll get a bill," she warned.

Nick shrugged, smiling. "Not a problem."

"Okay." She looked up at the waiter and they proceeded to order a dinner with the seriousness and meticulousness of peace negotiations between warring nations. It took a while, but at the end, Parker was sure they'd have a taste of everything worth tasting.

The waiter bowed his head in respect and glided off.

"I think we'll be stuffed at the end of the meal." She'd ordered enough to feed a platoon.

"But we'll probably be happy," he offered.

"Oh yeah."

He brought her hand to his lips. "I'm already happy and haven't eaten a bite."

His mouth was warm against her skin. He pressed a

kiss to the back of her hand, so fleeting she wasn't even sure it was there.

She nearly sighed, which maybe was gauche. But really—it was almost outrageously romantic. The beautiful evening, the elegant restaurant, the huge man courting her with soft words and gentle gestures. Not displaying any signs of jerkitude. He was interested in her and showed it every way there was but then she was interested in him, too.

Neither was pretending anything, which was fabulous. Just a healthy man and a healthy woman constantly finding things they liked about each other.

"Your Italian is excellent," he said, letting go of her hand. Her hand felt cold and alone, and she hoped he would hold it again soon. And then felt stupid. They'd need both hands to eat.

"Well, I've been living in Italy for four years and I work a lot with Italian archeologists. And I've been studying Latin since I was twelve years old. Italian is the only language directly descended from Latin without other influences."

"I'll bet you anything Aunt Caroline's Italian isn't good. Even after two years."

She smiled wryly, thinking of Aunt Caroline's incredibly mangled Italian. "No, it isn't. When she needs help, I lend a hand. Particularly outside the Consulate."

Nick topped up her glass. "Do you know any other languages?"

Parker picked up her glass by the stem, twirling it.

"Well...I'm a classicist, so ancient Greek and some modern Greek I picked up during summer seminars in Thessaloniki. My French isn't bad, and I have enough Spanish to survive in a Spanish-speaking country. And I speak a little Klingon, from my nerd days in boarding school. You?"

"Ukrainian and Russian. And I have enough Pashto to say, 'Put the gun down, motherfucker' and 'On your knees, hands behind your head.'" He smiled. "You'll pardon my French."

"Pardoned. I've learned quite a few strong phrases in Neapolitan dialect for when I'm in traffic. More or less the same, um, semantic field." Outrageously filthy expressions that would probably get her knifed if spoken to the driver, but which kept her sane when muttered in her car with the windows up.

"*Signori.*" Their elegant waiter appeared, pushing a trolley that smelled like heaven, if heaven were Naples.

They both straightened in their chairs as he unloaded a plate of pasta with clams, a plate of seafood risotto and a third plate of creamy pasta with provola cheese and potatoes which he placed in the middle. Then a thousand small plates of hors d'oeuvres—fried octopus, stuffed eggplant, tiny pizzas, steamed mussels with garlic, fried mozzarella.

Normally, all this food would have filled Parker with dismay. She had never had much of an appetite, and too much food on display made her nauseous. But not this time. Nope. Everything looked and smelled delicious, and her stomach just yawned wide open. She hadn't really eaten today, but it felt as if she hadn't *ever* eaten. As if she had just discovered food after years of fasting.

The *linguine alle vongole* was divine. Parker nearly moaned as she put a forkful in her mouth.

Nick did moan. "Oh man. You've got to try this. It's amazing." He held a forkful of his risotto in front of her lips. What could she do but open her mouth and let in luscious creaminess that tasted of the sea?

"It is amazing. Here, try this." She wrapped her linguine around her fork and held it up to his mouth. Oh God. The pasta was messy but he somehow managed to eat it neatly, looking straight at her. That firm mouth closed over her fork, and it was all too easy to imagine that mouth kissing her. And it would be as good as the pasta, she was sure.

Oh, dear. She was distracted by the fact that he seemed so eminently likeable, so strange for a tough guy. That's what he was, it was unmistakable. There was absolutely nothing of the metrosexual about him. His clothes were expensive, of fine material, serviceable, absolutely untrendy. No jewelry except an excellent watch.

His voice was very deep, but quiet. He did nothing to call attention to himself, but he was a presence, without seeming to want it.

Above all, he didn't brag about anything, though he had more reason than most to brag. He was part-owner of the most famous security company in the world, Black Inc., but he hadn't once tried to impress her with how powerful he was.

He didn't have to say he was powerful, though. Power came off him in waves. You could almost see them.

All of which made him incredibly attractive, as if he were a key to her lock, closed tightly all these years.

"Open up," he ordered, holding a forkful of the third pasta. Melted cheese and potatoes. She obeyed, closed her eyes and sighed.

"Right?" he said. "I am so glad this place does traditional food and not those little towers of crap chosen for color and not taste. One spoonful and it's gone."

"No nouvelle cuisine here." Parker looked at the table. "I don't think anyone could accuse this restaurant of short-changing the customers. There's enough food here to feed a platoon."

"More," he smiled. "Soldiers in the field eat MREs and they are small because they have to be carried. Little plastic packets filled with calorie dense food that tastes of cardboard."

"Well, so this dinner is a step up."

"Oh yeah." He stopped, those light blue eyes glowing. "A big, big step up. So tell me more about Romans planning for the apocalypse."

She cocked her head. "The apocalypse, in our acceptance of the term, of a breakdown in civilization, wasn't really a thing at the time. Apocalypse was a legend of the end of the known universe. There was the Scandinavian Ragnarok, and the Book of Daniel, but it was more a twilight of the gods. However, there was a generalized feeling that the center couldn't hold, though nobody could say out loud that Rome wasn't eternal. That Rome was eternal was a given. However, the number of people fleeing Rome increased every time a crazy emperor took the throne. As they did often. We have elections, but they had murder as a source of succession. I've got a little bevy of history nerds in Oxford digging up statistics for me, and when tracked on a graph, it's pretty clear."

"Did they say they were escaping crazy emperors?"

"Nope. That was an excellent way to get yourself killed and your entire bloodline eliminated. No, the usual excuse was retiring to the countryside for your health. Which, in a way of course, was true."

Nick was putting away an astonishing amount of food. It pleased her. He clearly hadn't had good food in a while. And there was plenty of it on the table. "Do you have your own plans if civilization falls?"

He looked at her carefully, studying her face. "I do," he said softly.

Yes. He looked like someone who would quietly plan for everything, including the fall of civilization. Maybe he'd give her a few pointers.

She smiled. "I have ten six packs of water and about five kilos of pasta in the house. I won't go far with those."

"Nope. Not far at all." He shook his head. "Is there anything I can help you with?"

Nick held up some more of his risotto to her mouth. Hmm. God, it was good. She chewed. Swallowed. Heaven.

"You mean with doomsday supplies? I have limited storage space. Not too sure I could follow your advice."

"No, I mean right now, with your project."

She started to shake her head then stopped.

He picked up on it immediately. Leaned forward. "Yeah? There is something? Not too good at Greek or Latin or even history, but I can carry bags for you. Be your water bearer." He flexed his biceps. "Big and strong. Will carry anything for you. Happy to."

Man, that flexed biceps was something else. Huge, heavily veined. He could probably carry a water tanker.

"Nice thought, but no. I don't really need for you to carry anything. However—"

"Yeah, ask me anything." He leaned even further forward, until their noses almost touched. "I want to help."

"Well, as I said, a Roman villa has been discovered near the Campi Flegrei in a huge archeological park. It's a real big find—an intact villa with one room beautifully frescoed. And there are documents in the villa. The owner was high up in Roman politics under the Emperor Caligula, and he left behind a sort of diary of political events. And it was clear he thought bad things were coming. A lot of important businessmen communicated with him, and he was giving advice. Most of the advice was—get out while you can."

"Sounds good."

"Yes. And I think I can anchor a segment of the book and the documentary on this Roman villa."

"Sounds great," Nick said, angling his head. "But? There's got to be a but here."

"Here's the thing, and I'm going to sound like the

world's biggest wuss. There's a work stoppage at the dig. Not a strike, that doesn't sound good, so they don't call it that, they call it a work stoppage. But it's a strike and everyone is staying home. It's been ongoing for a week and will last at least another two weeks. It's a little eerie out there, completely on my own. I'd be really glad of some company. I know it sounds—"

"God. Yes." Nick's smile was gone and he looked actually alarmed. She could see the whites of his eyes. "Yes, I'll accompany you. Even if I didn't want to—and I do—I would because you can't go out to some empty countryside on your own. Someone who looks like you—" he stopped suddenly and bit his lips.

"Someone who looks like me?" Parker cocked her head.

"Sorry. Sorry, not sorry." Nick took her hand again. "You know what I mean. And you know you're extraordinarily beautiful. To a certain kind of man that makes you extra tasty prey. As if being alone in the countryside weren't enough. You know I'm right."

Parker wanted to be pissy about it, but she couldn't because he was right. Everyone thought being attractive was this huge *thing,* but it was often a burden, and it did make her a target.

"I'll confess these past two days I did feel uncomfortable. And I'd be happy for the company. I'd feel safer, and I could concentrate on what I'm there to do instead of keeping an ear out for intruders. So thanks. And—would you mind driving? Neapolitan traffic just wears me down."

"Fine. This is nothing compared to places I've driven, where traffic lanes are just a suggestion and everyone is armed. Happy to drive."

She blew out a breath. "Actually, if you don't mind, I could go over my notes during the drive."

He smiled.

Just the sight of him there reassured her that she'd be able to make good use of her time. So big and so strong. Someone who had the personality to back up all that strength. Not a wuss. Parker had dated a few men with gym-honed muscles who'd melt at the first sign of trouble.

She was absolutely sure that Nick wouldn't melt. He was like a rock—unmeltable, uncrackable. If she lived to be a hundred, she'd never forget how incredibly solid Nick had felt in the earthquake.

It *had* been a little creepy being out at the dig on her own. More than a little, actually. The dig itself was in an isolated part of the archeological park, several kilometers in length. There was one guard manning a guard hut at the entrance to the park, but he arrived late, left early, and had a lunch hour that lasted several hours. She was all alone.

And now she wouldn't be anymore.

"Didn't you say you had a couple more days doing your field work?" he asked.

"Well, yes, but I don't want to monopolize your time."

"Whoa. Not a problem." His head reared back. "My time is yours. So tomorrow's Friday, can you complete your work there with tomorrow, Saturday and Sunday? Because if you need Monday, too, I'd have to notify your Aunt Caroline."

She shifted things in her head. It was definitely doable. "Yeah, I can. Particularly if I'm not worried about being bothered." She owed him a warning. "It will be boring for you, though. You should know that. I'll be taking photos and notes, and you'll just be standing around."

His eyes sharpened. "I'll be far from bored, trust me on this."

She smiled. "Well, I'll be very happy to have you drive and sort of be my guard dog, believe me. And I'll owe you, big time. If you are free for dinner tomorrow night, I'd like to invite you out. My treat."

"Love to, it's a date. But there's no question of you paying. Just couldn't do it. My mom would have my hide if she ever found out."

She rolled her eyes. "Come on. Please? You're going to be helping me."

He sighed. "Ask me anything else, but not this. Again, my mother would kill me."

The chances of Nick's mother finding out who paid for what were infinitesimal. But Nick, though smiling, looked adamant. He was not going to give up on this. But she couldn't just accept all that help and let him pay for dinner. It felt lopsided and put her deeply in his debt.

She watched him. He was comfortable under her scrutiny, calm and sure of himself. "Well, would you accept a dinner invitation at my house? Would that deprive you of your man card?"

Nick suddenly straightened, eyes wide. "You cook?" he breathed.

Parker was amused. "You made that sound as if I said I could fly to the moon. Of course I can cook. And I'm a decent cook. Nothing too fancy though."

He shook his head. "God, I don't need fancy. I haven't had a home-cooked meal in oh," he looked up toward the sky. "Maybe in at least a year and a half. My meals have been at crappy diners or MREs. Meals Ready to Eat, remember?" he added, noting her blank look. "Absolute poison for anyone who likes food. They are tasteless, manufactured to last years and could probably survive a nuclear blast. Gum you up good, too."

"Ack." Sounded awful. "I'm doubly sorry that the food at the Consulate was so bad, then."

He covered her hand with his. "I'm not. This meal more than makes up for that. I haven't eaten like this in a long time. And I haven't had such good company in a long time. Tonight's a real treat."

Parker looked at Nick. Really looked at him. And saw beyond the attractive face and tough, outsized body. Saw beyond the veneer of a wealthy, successful businessman who traveled the world.

She saw a lonely man, who had a tough job, and whose life held very few comforts. She was almost certain he had no one at home, if he even had a real home and not some corporate headquarters somewhere. He'd said he lived in London because it was a convenient time zone and that he was rarely there.

There didn't seem to be a woman in his life. There was just something about him that said he wasn't a cheater, a player. God knows she'd dated plenty of those and they had tells. Things they wouldn't talk about. Skirting some subjects. If you knew what to look for, you could tell.

But Nick was what he appeared to be—a highly successful single businessman in a hard business that required constant travel to unsavory places.

And she slipped, a little. That wall she'd had around herself since she was a girl developed a crack, opening up. New feelings started slipping in, feelings she'd never had before, centering around Nick.

She liked this man. A lot.

She put her other hand over his. "Tomorrow night I'll make you something you'll like."

His eyes caught hers. He said, voice low, "I already do."

Parker could almost feel the world disappear beyond his broad shoulders. Fade into nothing. The other diners, the glittering city, Vesuvius, the Bay. Poof! Gone. There was only Nick.

Parker startled when the waiter appeared, holding a huge platter. "*Signori. Ecco a voi.*"

NICK NEARLY JUMPED when the waiter suddenly appeared. Nick never jumped, never startled. Everything that could happen to him had already happened, except dying. He was immune to surprises, or so he thought. But there he was, drowning in the most beautiful pair of eyes he'd ever seen. Endless pools of cobalt blue, completely lost in them when all of a sudden, this guy pops up and pulls him out of ParkerWorld and oh, man was it a wrench.

To his utter surprise, he *resisted* coming back into the world. Nick was an ex-soldier, current security specialist, a warrior down to his bones. He lived in the real world, not some imaginary place with rainbows and unicorns and chirping birds. He never needed to be brought back into the world. He lived in the real world, warts and all, for better or worse, all the time.

So having lost himself even for a moment in amazingly beautiful eyes was unheard of for him.

Even worse, he liked it there.

He liked being immersed in ParkerWorld, with a beautiful, fascinating woman. It was a hell of a lot better than his world, full of violence and greed and hatred.

This was serious stuff. He'd be worried that he was losing his edge, except he was really enjoying himself and for the moment didn't care.

It had been a long, long time since he'd enjoyed himself.

So when the waiter showed up and brought him back into himself and into the real world, he just sat back and let Parker deal with it.

The waiter held out an enormous oval serving dish covered in a white crust. He laid it on a trolly and expertly broke the crust, revealing a huge fish, which he filleted, plating large chunks of white flaky fish. He spoke to Parker, with a question in his voice.

She smiled. "The waiter wants to know if he can dress the fish for you. Which means some olive oil and lemon."

At that moment, with Parker smiling at him, the twinkling lights of the harbor in the distance, the stars coming out, the waiter could have poured shit covered in glitter over the fish and he'd have nodded yes, happily. Lemon and olive oil sounded great.

"Sure. I don't think I've ever seen fish cooked in salt. Doesn't it become salty?" Truth was, he didn't care. He was having a real good time. The fuck did he care about salty fish?

The waiter was doing his best to keep up a professional demeanor, but he kept sneaking glances at Parker like he had when Parker had ordered their dinner.

Parker spoke briefly to the waiter, who took his time answering, never taking his eyes off her. Parker didn't seem to notice, or maybe she did. Maybe she was used to men not taking their eyes off her and had learned long ago not to pay attention.

Nick found it hard to imagine a straight guy with all his hormones not staring at her.

Parker turned to Nick with a smile. "The fish won't be salty, promise. The salt forms a crust that keeps the moisture in. You'll like it. And the greens are local to here, called *friarielli*. They are bitter, but good. And the potatoes are roasted with rosemary and oregano."

"Sounds good."

Nick enjoyed everything, including the bitter greens which were surprisingly good. He wasn't much for bitterness, life being bitter enough as it was. But these were tasty, cooked in a garlic sauce.

There was silence as they ate. This level of food deserved attention. Parker's appetite ran out before his did. He was still going strong when she laid her fork across her plate and sat back. It felt like forever since he'd had decent food. And here he was eating food of this quality with an amazing dinner companion like Parker, surrounded by the beauty of Naples.

Life had been pretty harsh these past years and now life was trying to make it up to him at every level.

"Ahh. This is really good stuff." He put down his fork and smiled at Parker. "So, when is your next book due?"

"Well." She sighed and took a sip of her wine. "It's due next April. The problem is that my production company wants the documentary to come out at the same time as the book. It's hard to get the dates to mesh. The production company sort of speaks a different language from the publishing house." She smiled. "Sorry. Those are first world problems, I'm sure you face much worse in your job and don't want to hear about mine."

"Yeah, I've faced worse, but that doesn't mean I'm not interested in your problems. Actually, I find them fascinating. Probably because I couldn't write a book if you put a gun to my head. It feels like magic."

Parker turned her head, fixed those twin cobalt headlights on him. "That sounds like the way I feel about how you negotiate Neapolitan traffic. Like magic."

Nick met her gaze. Held it. "I guess right now we're both touched by magic."

There was no way she could miss his meaning. She nodded. "Yeah," she said softly.

Damn right. Something was happening here, and it had never happened to Nick before. He'd been attracted before, plenty of times. Maybe not with this degree of intensity, but he'd had his share of infatuations. He liked women, a lot. Not just for sex, though that was always fun. He liked their soft voices, and gracefulness and different take on things. He lived in a man's world of iron and steel, and softness was precious and rare.

But this—this was something else. This was all of that cranked to eleven. Nick could almost see the lines of attraction in the air, like iron filings over a magnet. Parker was fascinating and intelligent—certainly better educated than he was—and incredibly talented. And that other-worldly beauty that was entirely natural.

An image sprang full blown in his head. Parker in the morning in bed, after a night of sex. Already full lips rosy and swollen from his mouth. He kept his eyes on her face, but he had excellent peripheral vision. He could tell her breasts were small but full and absolutely perfect. When they woke up, her nipples would still be cherry red because he couldn't imagine not licking them, sucking on them for hours. Between her legs, she'd be soft and wet and a little swollen because fuck, once he got in, he wasn't getting out for a long, long time.

Shit, he'd given himself a boner. Not the hopeful half woodie he'd had all evening, but the real deal, hard as a club and almost painful. He had to get rid of it, fast. First of all, because he was wearing lightweight trousers, and if she looked down, she could see it. And secondly, because women had the spooky ability of catching things in the air, and he was sure she would soon realize he had a hard-on. After which he could kiss this relationship goodbye. What woman wanted a randy guy who couldn't control himself and got wood at a restaurant, of all places?

Nick was thirty-eight years old, and this was the first time since freaking high school he couldn't control his dick. And here he was, losing control of his dick with the most attractive woman he'd ever been out with and that he wanted to see again. And again and again and again.

This had to stop. Right fucking now.

Nick took a deep breath and sat back in his seat, the picture of someone who'd eaten well and was stretching a little. He looked out to sea as if enjoying the view—which was spectacular—and thought of a village in Afghanistan after the Taliban had gone through. Nothing was left alive, not even the dogs and the chickens and goats. The ground had been soaked with blood. Then he thought of Ahmed. Everyone had been fond of him, he'd been so bright and friendly. He thought of his last glimpse of Ahmed, just before some fuckhead in another building blew him up. That small face looking so sad...

He had a lot of getting-rid-of-wood memories but those two were top of the line and they worked.

He'd got himself under control.

He poured another half-glass for Parker. She wasn't driving so she could indulge. "Speaking of your books, I never told you how much I enjoyed *The Smiling People*. As soon as I saw the documentary, I ordered the book on my tablet and read it in a couple of days. It was amazing. You write beautifully. I honestly don't know which I enjoyed more, the documentary or the book."

Parker sipped and a blush rose to her cheeks. She had remained indifferent to compliments to her beauty but compliments to her work made her blush. Oh God, he slipped a little deeper into infatuation. She had nothing of the coyness of a beautiful woman.

He'd dated good-looking women, and there was usually a background hum of *how'm I doing?* going on. *Am I beautiful enough? Are you paying me enough attention? If I tilt my head just so, you can admire my profile. Your last compliment was half an hour ago, I need another one. Quick.*

All that.

But nothing like that with Parker, who was by a factor of ten the most beautiful woman he'd ever been out with or even seen. She didn't want or need compliments on her looks. But she did appreciate compliments on her work. And rightly. What he'd read and seen represented hours and days and months and years of very hard work. Like a SEAL who didn't need compliments on his physique. It was earned, fought for. It was what a SEAL could do that was important, not what he looked like.

"Thanks for that." She looked down at the tabletop. She was self-assured, but at that moment she looked a little shy. "I appreciate it."

"No need to thank me. You earned it. You could tell that there was a ton of research behind it, but it was thoroughly readable. Do you have a list of future books in your head?"

She looked at him carefully as if judging whether he really wanted an answer. Yeah, he really did.

"Are you sure you want to know?"

"Absolutely sure."

"Okay. After *Apocalypse Then,* I was thinking of writing about Justinian's Plague. Don't know if you've ever heard of it."

He frowned. "Well, me not having heard about something historic isn't a sign of anything but my ignorance. But no, never heard of it."

"Don't worry. Not too many people have. And yet, it was the first world-wide pandemic that we know of. Some scholars say it was the first outbreak of bubonic plague, though some think it was smallpox. It is estimated to have killed something like fifty million people, about twenty-five percent of the world population. This would be around 550 AD."

"Fascinating." Nick stared. "That sounds really timely. And it would sell tons. This is fun. Anything else up your sleeve?"

She blew out a breath. "The Ninth Legion."

"Wait. I know that one. It disappeared, right?"

She nodded, "Over five thousand men. Gone. In a military culture that tracked the number of bread rolls. An absolute mystery."

"Wasn't it in England when it was lost?"

"That's the theory. They crossed Hadrian's Wall into Caledonia—what is now known as Scotland. Where resistance to Rome was fierce. Nobody really knows what happened, though there are a lot of theories. You were a military man, right?"

"For twelve years, yeah. Six years as a Navy SEAL."

"So maybe I'll use you as a military consultant. You'll understand military weaponry and tactics better than I ever could. I'll credit you in the acknowledgements."

He grinned. "Oh man, yeah. Count me in. That would be great." The whole idea tickled him. Being a consultant for a book on one of the great historical military mysteries. Getting named in the book. "My mom will be delighted that I got my name in a book. She thinks I am a barbarian. She's not wrong."

"No, no. You're not a barbarian. Far from it."

Parker covered his hand with hers. Her hand was soft and warm, and he never wanted her to lift it. He was listening to her words, but they came from far away. His hand buzzed where she touched it, like a mild electric shock.

Without even thinking about it, he covered her hand with his and the buzz increased. He looked at their two hands, hers slim and elegant, long fingered. A pianist's hand. His hands looked like blunt instruments of war.

Not too far from the truth.

That buzz was stronger now.

She said something, and he couldn't hear the words. All he could see was those amazing eyes and those luscious lips moving.

Finally, she smiled and withdrew her hand. He missed it. Some crazy connection was broken and the world rushed back in.

"—like?"

"What?"

Maybe Parker was used to men zoning out on her because she simply repeated what she'd said. "I said, what would you like? They're all good."

What was she—oh. The waiter had arrived while he'd been spaced out and had slid a big hand-painted oval platter full of desserts on the table.

Fuck. If this had been like most of the places he'd been stationed, someone could have slid a platter of grenades before him, and he wouldn't have noticed.

Parker was messing with his head. And she wasn't doing it on purpose, wasn't even aware of it.

She was smiling at him, serving fork in hand, over a platter of what looked like an amazing array of incredible desserts. One looked like a tan mushroom. Or a very strange dick.

"What's that?" Nick asked.

Her smile broadened and she cut the mushroom into

one large piece, the other much smaller. "It's a baba." The larger piece was deposited on his dessert plate. "Try it, you'll like it."

She watched as he put a bit in his mouth and laughed. "There you go. Great, isn't it?"

It was a delicate cake soaked in alcohol. "Rum?"

"Good for you. Yes, it's called a *Baba a rum*, a local specialty. Do you like it?"

It was amazing. Nick finished his portion in a couple of bites, hoping no cop stopped him as he drove home because there was enough rum in it to fell a horse.

"And now this." Parker put a triangular shaped pastry made of a billion layers folded over each other on his plate.

"I know this one, they were at the hotel breakfast buffet this morning. But I was in a hurry and didn't try it."

"Now's your moment," she smiled, and he cut a slice of the fragrant, crumbly pastry. "That's called a *sfogliatella*, which means many-layered."

"Mm." Nick was too busy chewing to answer. It was almost better than the Baba, filled with a fragrant creamy filling. It was gone in an instant. Then he looked at her plate, frowning. "I'm not eating another bite until you have something."

Parker laughed. "Yes, mom. Sorry. I was busy watching you."

"Glad to be a source of entertainment. But watch me while eating something. You're a writer. You can do two things at the same time."

"Yes, sir," she said, amused, and bit into her much

smaller piece of Baba. When she'd finished it, she cut out a large piece of a small pie. "Here, try this."

He did and his eyes widened.

"Yep." She smiled. "That's *pastiera.* Made of wheat berries. Very good."

It was. But there was a problem. "You're not eating any. That's not good."

She sighed. "Much as I'd love to, there simply isn't room. And besides, I am familiar with all of these sweets. The fun is watching you eat them for the first time." She loaded something else on his plate. A pretty pale-yellow mound. She pointed to it.

"I obey," he said, though even he was starting to be full. But man...the mound was creamy and lemony and delicious. He grinned, hoping the icing wasn't stuck to his teeth.

Parker smiled back at him. "That's called *Delizia al limone.* Lemon delight."

"In the military, there's a saying that's used a lot. Do the hard thing." He dug in. "Look at me. Doing the hard thing."

She laughed and Nick held his breath for a moment. She laughed like she seemed to do everything. Whole-heartedly and without pretense. That long white throat tipped back, eyes closed.

Her eyes opened unexpectedly, and she found him staring at her. He was so busted, so he just kept staring.

Her eyebrows lifted in an unspoken question.

"You should laugh more often," he said.

Parker sighed. "You don't know me well enough to know if I laugh often or not, though I have been told I am too serious. Sorry."

She'd taken it as criticism and the last thing Nick wanted was for her to feel he disapproved of her. He liked everything about her.

"No, I'm sorry. That was a stupid thing to say. I really do apologize."

"It *was* a stupid thing to say. If for no other reason, because a lot of women have to hear men tell them to smile more often. It's tedious. But I forgive you, because you did make me laugh."

"It's not a laughing world."

"No," she agreed. "It's not. Which is why it's so great to be light-hearted every once in a while."

"Yeah." God knows he hadn't had many light-hearted moments these past years.

And—though she presumably hadn't been in war zones —Nick had a flash of insight into this stunning, mysterious beauty.

She wasn't happy. A slight melancholy air surrounded her. She was fulfilled, doing work she enjoyed and was incredibly successful. But she had no family and clearly was used to being on her own and had been on her own since she was a child. He'd gone from a tightly knit family to the close bonds of the military, where hundreds of highly effective and dangerous men had his back at all times.

For no reason that he could see, this remarkable

woman was...alone. A woman like Parker, alone in this world—he couldn't believe it.

If he lived to be a thousand years old, he'd never forget her telling him, as if it were nothing, that she was receiving hate mail, yet had no one protecting her.

Man, if a woman of his were threatened, Nick would track the guy threatening her down and make him sorry. *Really* sorry. He wanted to do that now, for fuck's sake. Parker wasn't his woman, true, but...

Yet.

A voice whispered deep inside him.

The waiter rolled up with a huge liqueur cart, bottles rattling.

Parker smiled at Nick. "It's usual after a big dinner to have a digestive liqueur. Lots of people take *limoncello* because it's well known, but I'd recommend a *nocino*. A liqueur made from walnuts and not as sweet as a limoncello, but very pleasant."

Nick was tempted, but... He held up his hands. "Driving. But you go ahead and tell me if you like it."

She nodded at the waiter and pointed to a tall, slender brown bottle with a hand printed label. He poured the dark brown liquid into a small tulip glass, told her something, then looked questioningly at Nick. Nick shook his head, and the waiter rolled his cart away.

She tasted it and sighed. "It's great. The waiter said the chef's mother made it. I think it's one of those recipes that takes days. Sorry you're not drinking it."

"Leave a drop or two in the bottom." He liked the idea of drinking from her glass.

They both looked out over the Bay. There were fewer boats and, on the horizon, an enormous cruise ship that looked like the mother ship, huge, gaudy, brightly lit.

Vesuvius blocked the stars, a shadow in the sky.

The city was alive with light, the sounds of the traffic below, along the Bay, faint. Someone, somewhere, was practicing the violin and a woman's laughter suddenly erupted on the terrace.

All of it was good, was life itself, and so far removed from the places where Nick had spent the past couple of years. After sundown in those cities, there was little traffic, no women's laughter. Barely any lights on. Most people retreated behind the walls of their homes after dark.

Parker took a final sip and put the tulip glass down and slid it over to him. "You've got to try it. It's delicious." There was still a little liqueur in the bottom of the glass. "Walnuts steeped in alcohol and a ton of special spices."

Nick picked it up and drained it. He blinked. It was tart and intense with a touch of sweetness, very aromatic and perfect for an after-dinner drink. "Wow."

"Right? One of these evenings, we'll both take taxis so you can enjoy the wine fully and we'll have a nocino and maybe—" Parker suddenly stopped on an intaken breath and turned pink. "Sorry—"

"No. No. Don't be sorry." Nick put his hand on her arm. She was embarrassed that she'd assumed she'd be seeing him in the future. She didn't have to be embarrassed. She was going to be seeing as much of him as she could stand. "Consider my every moment not spent working for the Consulate at your disposal. As many dinners and lunches as you can bear."

Breakfasts, too, he thought, without saying it. But it was true. Just as soon as she said yes, they were going straight to bed. The sooner the better. His skin itched with the thought.

She'd thought she was presuming, but she wasn't. There was something here and he wanted—badly—to explore it. Maybe she did, too.

"Okay," she said softly. "Okay."

They nodded at each other. She was the first to break eye contact and looked around at the almost-empty terrace. Most of the guests had departed, even in Naples, where dinners usually started late. Nick was watching her, not wanting to take his eyes off her to check his watch. But he had a pretty accurate clock in his head, and he reckoned it was close to 1 am. Evening traffic along the bay had slowed down and the area had become quiet.

Time to leave.

He had no desire to leave. None.

He wanted to stay here forever. With Parker, on a terrace overlooking the sea with the stars shining down. Feeling excited and happy and...calm. Like he'd finally found something he didn't know he'd been looking for.

· · ·

IL TERRAZZONE. The restaurant was one of those Neapolitan institutions George normally only glimpsed when passing in a taxi—the kind with white table linens perfectly ironed, silver gleaming in soft candlelight, and an unspoken rule that only the wealthy and the glamorous dared enter.

The chosen.

Well, he was quickly becoming one of the chosen. He was rising, though making sure nobody noticed. His wardrobe was much better, but he made a point of saying he'd found a good, cheap tailor. Not that anyone noticed, really. At first, he splurged on some really good restaurants—though not *Il Terrazzone*—but he went alone and it got old.

No matter. Money in the bank soothed him.

It was essentially a matter of money. A normal meal at *Il Terrazzone* was apparently €200 a head and they were having a spectacular meal, so it was entirely possible Nikolai Garin was going to drop at least €500 tonight.

Garin could afford it. He could afford ten, a hundred times that, easily. He was part-owner of Black Inc., which everyone knew was a money machine and, apparently, he was also part-owner of another security company, the one that was tasked with working for the Consulate. He was drowning in cash. George wasn't drowning, but he was slowly coming up in the world.

But even with money, Parker Donovan wouldn't go out with him, look at him with soft eyes the way she was looking at Garin. The man who might drag George down.

George was in the cafè part of *Il Terrazzone*, where you could have a drink and a few *antipasti* for under €50. Above all, the cafè portion was hidden behind huge potted plants, so George could watch Garin and Parker without them noticing him.

They were at the best table in the restaurant, with the best view over the bay. Parker looked happy and relaxed, as if she belonged in the restaurant. Of course she did.

Rich background. Polished education—a PhD in Classical Studies, for fuck's sake. Author of a bestselling book and a successful Netflix documentary. Walking proof of everything George wasn't.

Once again, George was on the outside looking in. Always outside—all his life, looking through windows at people with better clothes, better blood, better luck.

But things had changed. He'd made sure of that. He had his app. His buyers of intel. His income had doubled, tripled and would triple again. He could afford good suits now. Good watches. He was rising, seizing the life others had denied him.

So why did he feel so damned small, watching Garin sit exactly where George had imagined himself—at Parker's side, while she glowed in candlelight?

Still, he was the one with the app, wasn't he? He was the one who could spy on the Consul.

And no one knew about his app.

It was well hidden. It would take someone like Garin to find it, and even then, there was nothing that tied his cell to the Consul's cell.

George had thought about removing the app while the security consultant was here, but that would require him actually having Munro's cell in his hands for about ten minutes. That would be more dangerous than the unlikely event of someone stumbling across his app.

George had put in a bid for the Dubai Embassy as his next posting. Now that was something to look forward to. Access to the cell of the Ambassador to Dubai was golden.

Garin said something, and Parker leaned forward to hear him better.

Garin sat as if the place belonged to him, his posture almost military. George had done his homework and Garin had been in the military almost twelve years. A fucking navy SEAL. Medals up the wazoo.

He was not Parker's type. Women like her preferred polished types but that wasn't Garin. Still, he had a powerful presence, and it pulled her in. Or maybe the money? Though she had plenty of her own. What the fuck?

It made him sick.

Parker had refused him over and over. He'd asked politely, discreetly. Drinks. Dinner. A simple walk along Via Caracciolo. She always smiled, but responded with something clipped in her tone. *I'm busy, George. Another time, George.*

Even if it was clear another time would never come. And here she was, out to dinner with a man she'd met this afternoon, leaning forward to hear whatever Garin had to say in his low, deep voice.

Watching them burned in his gut. Because this wasn't only professional now. Keeping his secret safe from the security pro. The security pro had everything George wanted—authority, respect, power and money.

And now Parker.

Garin leaned forward, said something. Parker laughed. She was so beautiful when she laughed. Their glasses touched lightly. A toast, their eyes holding just a moment too long. George looked away sharply, his throat raw with rage.

Garin looked around the restaurant casually, but he did that often. Keeping an eye on the terrain. George moved his head fully behind the huge leaves of the big plant next to his chair, so he was hidden from view.

But he'd seen enough. He called for the bill because there was one more thing to do tonight.

Parker didn't want the evening to end. Lots of times on dinner dates she nearly cracked her jaw suppressing yawns and had to stop herself from checking the time constantly.

Not now.

The evening flew by, easy and fun and exciting. Nick was really easy to talk to. So easy she never felt the time passing. Everything seemed to be enhanced—the food amazing, the wine exquisite, the gentle breeze off the sea a warm caress on her skin.

And the biggie, of course. Sexual attraction. Wild sexual attraction, by the time the evening was over. Every time Nick touched her, heat bloomed under her skin. She was probably stoplight red, though maybe that could be attributed to the wine and the spicy food.

She knew better. This wasn't the wine, it was the man.

This particular man. Tall, with immensely broad shoulders, heavily muscled, harsh features and on top of all that...interesting. He didn't in any way try to impress her. He didn't have to. He was impressive all on his own, by his very nature. He exuded power, but wasn't trying to overwhelm her in any way. Instead, he was super attentive and seemed to want to hear what she had to say.

Parker talked more to him about her projects that she had to any other human being, including her agent. Her agent was interested in the final product, so he could sell it. Nick really seemed interested in the process, too.

But the waiters standing around had a slightly impatient expression and they were the last clients on the terrace.

She turned to Nick. "I think it's time to go."

"Pity," he said.

Yeah. It was a pity. She nodded.

Nick got up and pulled out her chair as she stood up. Another really attractive trait.

Old fashioned manners, really odd in such a rough man. But that mother he claimed he was terrified of must have taught him well because he did things that men didn't do anymore. Stand up when she entered a room. Pull out her chair when she sat and when she got up. Listening to her. Refusing to even contemplate allowing her to pay. Granted, that last point was also a little annoying because she wanted to invite him out as thanks for keeping her company while she worked. But no.

He wouldn't let her pay.

It wasn't a question of him having more money, though he did. But she wasn't hurting, either. It was just that he'd looked genuinely distressed at the thought of her paying.

Nick cocked his arm, and she slipped her hand into the crook of his elbow. Again, that electric feeling as she touched steely muscles. He smiled down at her and took her hand, tucking it more firmly against him.

"One last look?" he asked quietly.

She nodded and they went to the edge of the huge terrace and leaned against the waist-high balcony, looking out over the Bay. Such beauty, such magic.

The lights of the city twinkled like scattered diamonds, tracing the winding streets and ancient buildings. Far below, the Bay of Naples stretched out like a great dark mirror,

The air was cool and carried the faint scent of saltwater mixed with the distant aroma of jasmine and citrus from the gardens below.

Nick sighed. "So beautiful."

It was. And it was the first time Parker had had a chance to share this beauty with someone who appreciated it. She'd been on a few dates with Neapolitan men who took it completely for granted.

The waiters were putting chairs on the tables, sweeping up. Parker glanced at Nick. "Our cue to leave."

They crossed the terrace arm in arm, and it wasn't until they were back on the street that Parker realized something. "Um, Nick?"

He turned to her, smiling. "Yeah?"

"We didn't—um, you didn't, you know...pay."

He patted her hand. "Don't worry. It's taken care of."

Oh. More magic. Did she want to know?

No. She didn't want to know.

Had he waved an enchanted wand? Somehow paid telepathically? Who knew? Who cared? If there was ever an evening for magic payments, pulling money right out of the air, it was tonight.

They started holding hands, quite naturally. Parker couldn't remember the last time she'd held hands with a man. With anyone, really. The last time she could remember holding hands with someone was crossing a busy street with a teacher when she was a child. It was incredibly intimate, and you had to move as a unit, not as two separate beings. His hand was warm, large, as hard as wood.

She got used to walking beside him, holding hands, very quickly. Like the most natural thing in the world. The air was soft and smelled of linden trees and jasmine and car exhaust, not unpleasant. The full moon had risen high in the sky, casting an unearthly silver glow over the streetscape.

She'd forgotten where they'd parked but he hadn't. Way too soon, they were at his car. He lifted her up, rounded the vehicle and slid behind the wheel.

He turned his head to look at her. "Home?"

Parker nearly sighed with longing. It had been a spectacular evening, and she didn't want it to end. The temptation was so strong to prolong the evening. She knew a jazz club near *Spaccanapoli* that was fabulous. Incredible music and excellent drinks. Or they could take a drive, it was a beautiful evening. But...she was an adult and had to work the next day. He'd volunteered to come along, too. Tomorrow would be a long, hot day out in the middle of nowhere and she should be rested up.

She didn't want to say it, but she did. "Home."

He said nothing, just put the vehicle in gear. You could barely hear the engine, and all the outside noises were screened out. It was like being in a bubble. In a bubble with someone else, someone absolutely fascinating. She couldn't remember when she'd been so attracted to a man. Every sense on alert, excitement skittering under her skin.

Because of course the big question was—should she invite him in? She'd like nothing more. The whole evening had been a huge turn-on. Her heart beat so fast, she couldn't seem to pull in enough air. Her breasts felt heavy. So very weird because she wasn't usually aware of her own breasts as separate entities. But there they were—on her chest, feeling bigger, nipples definitely aroused. And between her legs...well. Heat radiated from her sex, and she had to stop herself from fidgeting and crossing her legs.

Sex would definitely make her feel better.

This wasn't like her *at all*. She was incredibly picky, and she had to remind herself that every sex partner she'd ever had had turned out to be a disappointment. Too fast, too slow, too crass, too timid. Not enough, too much.

What to do?

Nick didn't need any instructions and was driving them straight to her place. It had taken her a week to memorize the route. They would be there in a minute or two.

Maybe she could invite him in and keep it casual, just to have more time in his company. She had a nice collection of home-made liqueurs, though he'd been pretty careful about alcohol consumption since he was driving.

Maybe ask him if he wanted an herbal tea? Parker often finished a meal with an herbal tea. Ginger, chamomile, fennel, peppermint, turmeric. Would he want one? He actually didn't look like an herbal tea kind of guy, but maybe out of politeness he'd accept a cup. Maybe not chamomile, maybe ginger?

Did she still have fresh ginger? She seemed to remember she'd run out and hadn't bought any. Maybe peppermint? She had several peppermint plants out on her little terrace, so...

The car stopped. "We're here," Nick said, and all those febrile thoughts bouncing like ping pong balls around Parker's brain stopped too, and her head was now filled with blank space. Nothing going on upstairs at all.

Utter silence in the car. She drew in a breath to speak, but had no idea what she wanted to say.

"Do you want to—"

"Yes," he said. "I do."

Parker blinked. "You do? You do what? I haven't even said anything."

His face turned to her, and he looked utterly serious. "Whatever it is you were about to say, the answer is yes. Would I like to—fill in the blank. Whatever the blank is, the answer is yes."

"Wow." She smiled. "That could be dangerous. What if I asked you to...I don't know. Swim across the Bay?"

"How far across is it?"

"Hmm. About ten miles, I think."

He thought for a moment. "Ten miles. Yeah, I've done that in training. It would be really tiring, and I wouldn't be laughing at the end, but I could do it in about three hours." His nose wrinkled. "Though I'm not sure how clean that water is."

"Not very. I wouldn't recommend it. Actually, what I was about to ask you was—would you like to come up for an herbal tea to finish the evening? I have chamomile, fennel..."

But he was already getting out of the vehicle and moving to her door.

She watched him as a deep thrumming began in her chest. She felt almost as if she were choking, only it didn't hurt. As he was rounding the vehicle, his eyes met hers through the windshield and it was like a punch to the stomach.

Then he was at her door, big hands up. She leaned down, placing her hands on those broad shoulders, letting herself fall forward, knowing he'd catch her.

He caught her.

She slid down his body, every nerve sensitized. Everything was in overload, and she couldn't speak. There was no breath in her body to speak. They walked up the little walkway in silence, Parker feeling excited and wary and everything in between. To her astonishment, when they got to the big wrought iron and glass front door, she couldn't fit the key to the lock. She couldn't even feel her hands.

Nick gently took the key out of her hands and opened up the big street door, reaching above her head to open it for her. Parker started deep breathing to get herself under control, then saw the elevator and indignation wiped away her excitement. It was an old building with an ancient wheezing elevator, a glass enclosed cabin in a wrought iron cage. And right now, a huge sign hung from the doorknob.

FUORI SERVIZIO

Out of order

"Oh!" She turned to Nick. "I'm so sorry. The elevator just goes on the blink from time to time. They keep promising to fix it but..." She blew out a breath in frustration.

Nick smiled. "Not a problem. It's two floors."

But she knew what that elevator out of order meant. She skirted the stairwell and, yup. There it was. A mess of shopping, at least ten plastic shopping bags. She bent to gather them all up.

"My next-door neighbor is an elderly lady. I told her that if she did heavy shopping and came home to find the elevator out of order to just leave her shopping here and I'd carry it up for her. It's happened a couple of times." She hefted the bags. "Feels like she did her weekly shopping this evening."

"Whoa. Let me." He took all the bags, holding them in one big hand. She protested that she could take half, but he didn't even answer, just started up the stairs. On her landing, he turned to her. "Now what? Where do we leave these?"

"On this floor, two doors down. Just leave them at the door."

"No one will steal them?"

"Nah. It's a nice building and everyone is fond of Mrs. Da Costa. She's pretty generous with her baked goods. No one will steal her shopping. What?"

Some strange fleeting expression crossed his face as he put down the shopping in a neat pile to the side of Mrs. Da Costa's door.

Nick straightened. "Well, this is really new to me. I've spent the past couple of years in places where if you meet a neighbor in the corridor, the first thing you do is you check his hands for a gun or a knife. My place in London is really upscale, but I have no idea who my neighbors are. Wouldn't recognize them. Certainly no one does anyone any favors. This is nice."

She smiled, recognizing what he was telling her. That despite his success, despite his money and power, he led an empty life. Certainly emptier than hers. Of course, it was hard to live in Naples and not make human connections.

Neapolitans basically forced themselves into your inner circle, though she, too, had empty spots.

"You should live in Naples. Or at least somewhere in Italy." She'd spoken thoughtlessly and immediately cringed. He could interpret that in a number of awkward ways. He could think she was questioning his life choices, choosing to live in terrible places. Or he could think she was damning his social skills. Or—and this was the worst—he could think she was encouraging him to move to Italy on the basis of a nice dinner.

Which she wasn't. Of course she wasn't. That would be crazy.

"I really should." Nick smiled down at her. "Be a big improvement."

She opened her door, wondering what was going to happen. Would he accept a cup of herbal tea and leave? Would they kiss? Would—

And then she didn't have to wonder at all because he kissed her, and the world stopped.

NEAPOLITAN STREETS WERE narrow and twisted. George had a FIAT 500, small and compact so he could navigate the streets. Garin had a huge SUV, but he managed just fine. George had put a tiny chrome tracker on the left back light of the SUV, almost completely invisible. It was small and didn't have much of a range, but it would do its job.

George kept himself three streets behind. But soon it

was clear where Garin was headed. To Parker's apartment on the Vomero.

He was driving Parker home. Was he going to spend the night? Parker was incredibly picky. Everyone said so. And from what George could tell she hadn't had any lovers. She wouldn't fuck Garin the night she met him, would she?

George didn't have to start tracking Garin right away.

Garin wasn't even starting the contract until Monday, so about the only things he could do was study the Consulate's floor plans and the organization chart. George was sitting pretty. The floor plans sure as hell weren't going to help find the leak, which was in Caroline Munro's phone, and his own bio was almost ridiculously uninformative.

Though George had no reason to track Garin so early, here he was, caught in the trap of his own obsession. He kept an eye on the GPS app glowing faintly on his phone's screen as his FIAT made its way through darkened streets, casting arcs of light against the stucco facades, watching cafès shuttering for the night.

And then the teardrop on the screen stopped.

George slowed, coasted, then pulled into a side street, and there it was. Garin's big SUV. Right in front of Parker Donovan's building. George knew where she lived. He'd driven by dozens of times, working up the courage to stop by. *I was in the area...*

But she probably wouldn't let him in the door.

She let Garin in the door.

George's throat closed.

Parker had refused him so many times. Almost a caricature of rejection. Cool and dismissive. And here Nikolai Garin shows up at a Consulate reception and she goes out to dinner that same evening and they were probably fucking right now.

George's hands tightened on the steering wheel, until his knuckles turned white. He sat frozen in his small FIAT until a passing scooter buzzing too close to him snapped him back to reality.

He had done everything right. Everything. He had crafted his new life, piece by piece. Clothes that finally fit him and looked good, a wallet thick enough to prove he wasn't just a petty functionary. He had risked far more than Garin. Risked prison, risked ruin. Yet—who was rewarded?

Not George. Never George.

Always men like Garin.

Men like Garin walked into a room and simply took what they wanted. Women. Respect. Money. As if the world owed it to them. And though George thought Parker was different, more refined, with better taste than most, she wasn't.

Garin wasn't coming back down from her place.

So—lesson learned. Monday morning he'd be back at the Consulate, friendly, helpful George, the pleasant cultural attaché. Smiling and dependable. Invisible.

And willing to sell anything at all to anyone who'd pay him.

Because people could underestimate him—but he was privy to secrets. He sold power. And nothing would stand in his way.

My God, the taste of Parker was heady. Nick wanted to take it slow, gentle kisses graduating to open mouth kisses but the instant that door closed behind them it was like being in a raging river, unable to stop.

He held her head still for his kiss. Her hair was warm, flowing over his fingers, and it was a little shock. Her hair was midnight black, you almost expected it to be cool, but it was warm, like her.

He only touched her head, with his hands and his mouth. He wasn't leaning against her, because he was fully aroused and had no idea if she was ready for that.

As far as he was concerned, he was ready—right now—to drop to the floor, rip her clothes off and unzip himself just enough to slam into her. The thought—the image—excited him and appalled him. You don't woo a woman like Parker by being a caveman. Which was a pity because he felt like a caveman. He was more aroused than he'd ever been with any other woman, but this was a woman he didn't want to scare, in any way.

When Parker's tongue stroked his, all the blood in his body pooled in his dick and he nearly came. Not good. Not good at all, because Parker deserved a partner who was in control of himself. Not some sex-crazed maniac.

Control. Fuck. He was nothing *but* control. He could

go for two days without water, a week without food, days without sleep. As a soldier, he was unstoppable, which wasn't possible without control.

But now control was slipping from his fingers.

His fingers were holding her head too hard. He slapped his hands on the wall beside her head and kissed her more deeply, fingers digging into the wall.

Parker licked inside his mouth, and he huffed out a breath. Lifted his head.

Oh God. How could she be even more beautiful? Cheeks a deep rose, eyes blazing blue, mouth slightly swollen and dark pink.

He leaned his forehead against hers.

"I wanted to do that from the first instant I set eyes on you."

"What? Kiss me?"

"Mhm." More than kiss her.

"I actually didn't think of kissing you, but I did think you were not obnoxious. Which is high praise for me."

"I'll bet you get a lot of come-ons."

She sighed. "And suggestive comments and sometimes pinches and copping feels."

Nick made a sound deep in his throat at the thought of someone pinching Parker.

She smiled. "Was that a growl?"

"Yeah. I hate the thought of that. Of someone making you uncomfortable. Maybe hurting you."

She laid a hand alongside his face. "Well you can rest

assured that you have always behaved like a perfect gentleman. I like that."

Then and there Nick made a vow to himself to be a gentleman. No matter what it cost him.

She smiled up at him. "I'll confess as we were driving across town, I was trying to think of a way to get you to come up with me."

Nick felt his eyes widen. *"Think of a way?"*

She nodded, watching him.

"Ahm...it wasn't hard. You offered me an herbal tea. You could have offered me cyanide, a bullet, barbed wire to sit on. I'd have come up. Easy."

She smiled. He pulled his hand away from the wall and ran the back of his fingers down her face. She was so fucking beautiful. Why was she so beautiful? Almost an extravagance. Her skin was so soft, her mouth so lush. Uptilted eyes so gemlike while also being intelligent.

He bent again and she lifted herself up and opened her mouth before his touched hers and they were in perfect alignment. His tongue touched hers and it was a straight electric line to his dick. When he lifted his head, her mouth was wet, lips a little swollen. Skin a little rosy. A woman who'd been kissed.

Absolutely irresistible.

He ran his hand down her neck. She had a beautiful neck. Beautiful skin. Damn. An image flashed in his head of a naked Parker, spread-eagled on a bed, after sex. After he'd feasted on her for hours.

He had to bring himself down a notch. He was almost

panting and he was completely aroused, and she could feel it because now he was pressed against her. He needed to feel her. She knew he wanted her, but he didn't have a clue how much she wanted him back. He hoped at least a fraction of how turned on he was.

Granted, it had been a while since he had had sex. He'd been in the badlands for a long, long time. So yes, he had pent up desire. But this wasn't pent-up desire, it was something different. Something bigger. As if he'd never had sex before and would die if he couldn't have her *now*.

This wasn't a way to start a relationship, and he realized this was what was happening. He'd never approached sex as anything but itself. An act. Pleasurable, but with a beginning, a middle and an end. Complete.

With Parker, he wanted more. He wanted this to be the start of something, but it wouldn't be the start of anything if he behaved like a starved wolverine. So just when he was as excited as he'd ever been in his life, he needed to be the gentleman she wanted. Or, if not a gentleman, at least with a modicum of control.

He huffed out a breath.

Parker was looking at him, head to one side. No doubt wondering what the crazy guy was up to, standing there staring at her.

He had moves. He really did. He'd been having sex for a long time. He knew what he was doing with women, so why was he so clumsy now?

Because he cared.

God. That wasn't helping.

Just ask, he thought. "Are we—are we taking this to the bedroom?"

"If you want to," she replied softly.

If he wanted to? Fuck. Did he want to breathe?

"Um. Yes."

She stood there, watching his eyes, as if gauging whether he was telling the truth. Well, she could look all she wanted because *hell yeah*, he wanted to take this to the bedroom.

Parker walked them into the bedroom and turned on a small brass lamp. The bedroom was almost feminine overkill. Flowered sheets on a four-poster bed, a big mirror with an elaborate frame, a crystal vase with some fresh roses, a couple of pieces of antique furniture, little silver bowls with flower petals everywhere. It smelled of flowers and fresh linens. God knows he'd spent enough time in terrible fourth world hotels where the bedsheets smelled like goats slept in them.

Parker turned to him, relaxed. Hands down by her side, watching him. Nick wasn't relaxed. Particularly a special part of him wasn't relaxed.

In none of the fevered images he had in his brain of them having sex were there clothes. So he had to do something. Parker wasn't making a move, so he had to do it, and he had to move normally. No ripping or tearing. Nope. That was an expensive dress.

Nick reached out, touched her neck. Oh God. She closed her eyes and tilted her head. He smoothed his hand over her shoulder and reached behind her. Ah. He managed to find the tab of the zipper of her dress without fumbling. The god of soldiers watching over him.

He pulled down slowly, watching her carefully. The zipper ran down the length of her back. The dress—the exact color of her eyes—loosened. He pulled the two parts down until the top rested on her hips. She had on a cream-colored lacy bra. She made no move to cover herself, just watched him watching her. He reached again behind her, and though he prided himself on being good with his hands, his hands now felt clumsy, too big.

But he eventually got her bra undone and swiped it off and oh God.

Parker was watching his face, so she had to understand his reaction. Perfect breasts, like a marble statue, only he could see a slight heartbeat in her left breast.

This wasn't a marble statue, this was a living woman. Smart and bright and amazing. She tasted perfect, too, he discovered when he licked and kissed her breasts. Like a salty vanilla ice cream cone. He heard her give a big sigh as she clutched his shoulders.

"Nick," she whispered.

"Right here," he whispered back.

He pushed her dress down and straightened, looking at her, dressed only in lacy underpants and black sandals. The underpants fell to her ankles, and he kneeled, picking up one foot after the other, removing the underpants and sandals and then fuck. There she was, naked. She dazzled him.

Nick held her shoulders as he looked at her.

"How can you be perfect all over? Even your toes are beautiful."

Parker smiled slightly. "I'm at a slight disadvantage here."

Nick wasn't feeling too bright and at first didn't understand. Then a light went on in his head. "Oh!" She wanted him to strip too.

God yes.

If there was a land speed record for stripping, Jesus, he topped it. Everything flew off. There was a weird moment when he pulled down his trousers and briefs and his dick sprang out...they both looked down. It looked like a club hanging off his body, red and inflamed. It barely looked like a human organ.

Nick looked up. "I want you," he said hoarsely.

She smiled at him. "I can, um, see that," she said, voice soft.

Nick picked her up and just managed to refrain from throwing her on her pretty bed with flowered sheets and ruffles and a billion pillows. At the last minute, he lay her down gently, stood and just looked, dazzled.

So incredibly beautiful, all over, head to toe. She was like a prize he'd won. He'd spent years and years in terrible places with terrible people doing terrible things and now this was his reward, but something he'd have to treat gently, and cherish.

Inside, it was like a battle was playing itself out, because he was a warrior and he had a warrior's blood. And that blood was up. There was a part of him that wanted to mount Parker, pull her legs apart, enter her and start fucking her, hard. He was as aroused as he'd ever been and that would get it out of his system.

But this was *Parker*, and he didn't want to get her out of his system. He was a modern man, and he didn't want to conquer her. He wanted her with him, every step of the way.

Was she with him?

Only one way to find out.

He circled her delicate ankle, opened his hand, ran it slowly up her calf, the skin so soft and smooth it almost seemed like another material, not human flesh. Up her thigh, slowly.

"Open your legs." She obeyed instantly and was just as beautiful between her legs as she was elsewhere. Soft, dark pink lips surrounded by a sable cloud.

Nick touched her there and she sighed. He did, too, because she was wet. This was going to work. He circled her opening gently and her thighs trembled. One finger in her, two, moving in and out.

Parker's eyes were half closed and all you could see was a cobalt blue shard of color. His fingers moved in and out, harder now and faster. He bent to lick her left nipple, the one where he could see her heartbeat. As his fingers moved deeper, faster, he sucked at her nipple, feeling it growing hard, like a little pearl.

Parker was holding his wrist, her head tipped back against the wall of pillows. His fingers moved faster, faster and suddenly she gave a cry, and he could feel her contracting against his hand, her belly muscles pulling.

Nick opened his fingers and entered her, feeling her pulling against him. He lay on her, kissing her deeply, not moving, until her climax was over. The first but not the last.

When she relaxed, thighs falling to the sides, he pressed hard inside her and began moving.

CHAPTER
Six

Something soft against his cheek. Something that smelled really good.

Nick had a soldier's reflexes and came awake instantly, always. Fully oriented, fully ready for battle. Sometimes with gun in hand. The world was a dangerous place, and you could never let down your guard.

But now? Nah.

He came awake in small swoops. Softness. A really nice smell. Though his eyes were closed, sunshine painted the inside of his lids a golden glow.

Another soft touch and his eyes opened, briefly. Man, his lids felt heavy. He did not want to wake up.

Lips kissed his cheek.

"I wish I could let you sleep, but we have a long day ahead of us."

A few facts seeped into his sex-and sleep-soaked brain. He was not in one of his hardship posts. The bed was exceedingly comfortable, and he felt really good. It wasn't his London flat, either. His bed there was hard as a board and smelled of professional dry cleaning.

And sure as hell nothing soft touched his cheek.

He opened his eyes and met amazing blue eyes.

"Hi," Parker said softly. "Sorry to—"

He hooked a hand around her neck, pulled her to him and kissed her. It felt familiar and new. They'd kissed all night, but they hadn't kissed in the morning. It had a hotness all its own. Nick wrapped his arms around her back and turned with her in his arms. She was under him, that slender elegant frame his to explore. His hand went slowly up her side until he was cupping her breast.

Oh yeah.

Parker smiled against his mouth. "Much as I'd like to continue this, I'm afraid you're going to have to get up. If you want to take a shower, I laid out a towel for you. When you get out, breakfast will be ready. It won't be as elaborate as the breakfast at your hotel, but I think you'll be satisfied."

And she slithered out from under him and was gone.

Christ. He missed her, missed the feel of her in his arms. But good things for him were in store. Just sitting across the table from her would be fantastic, let alone if she fed him.

Nick padded naked across her bedroom. He glanced outside the window. It was a glorious day, the sky bright bright blue. On the horizon, the Bay was a flat blue table with toy boats sailing across it. It was going to get hot. He was going to have to make sure Parker slapped on sunscreen.

Her bathroom smelled of her and it gave him a half-boner. His dick hopefully stuck straight out. Having loved what it did last night and wanting more, more, more.

Well, he told his dick, forget about it. For now.

The bathroom was small, pretty, old-fashioned. With one shower spout that got the job done. His London flat bathroom was huge, had acres of marble everywhere and the shower had eight shower heads. It had taken him ten minutes to figure out how the settings worked when he moved in.

And he was someone who'd managed to learn to use a Chinese GPS. Fast. Under fire.

Parker's shower was self-explanatory and worked just fine. The towel was great—big and fluffy and smelling of lavender.

While he was showering, Nick was torn between dragging Parker back to the bed and having more sex. As much as they could stand.

Door number one.

Door number two was being a big boy and accepting that sex wasn't going to happen right this moment. It would happen later. When they came back and she fed him. Including tiramisu.

Right now it was breakfast and a day in Parker's company.

And as he was toweling off, Nick had a sudden stab of insight. He didn't have many of them, he knew. He was a totally fact-based man without much introspection. But he realized what was different about the night they'd spent together.

He wanted more. But not just of the sex.

His adult life had been spent on missions with infrequent down times. His missions were in sex-free zones of the world. Not to mention everyone's dick stayed down in danger zones.

So when he could have sex, he tended to fill up.

His last lover had been an analyst for the Financial Times in Hong Kong, a year ago. They were staying in the same upscale hotel and had met at the hotel bar. They both had four-day layovers. They spent those four days in bed, even eating room service meals on the bed, with a DO NOT DISTURB sign on the door.

They'd both been sore at the end of the four days.

She left early on the morning of the fifth day, leaving a nice note.

He never did find out her last name. He could have discreetly inquired at the hotel desk. Go Solutions was a corporate client, and they would have told him.

But he didn't. It had been fun, but it hadn't been more than the sex.

With Parker, he couldn't wait to spend more time with her, in and out of bed. And there'd be time. He'd make sure of it. This didn't end here.

He dressed and walked into the small kitchen. Parker turned and saw him and blushed.

"Hey," she said.

He walked over and kissed her. "Hey."

A moka pot started boiling on the stove, and the smell of freshly brewed coffee filled the room. She smiled at him. "Breakfast is ready. Go sit down and I'll join you. Crazy after last night's meal, but I'm actually hungry."

They'd burned a bazillion calories last night, but Nick said nothing. There was a small table set for breakfast right under a window that let in a huge amount of light.

Nick stood until Parker brought in the moka and sat down. He leaned back and looked at the table. "Really nice," he said.

There were a pretty cream-colored tablecloth and cream-colored napkins. A breakfast set of dishes with a light green rim and green mugs.

The table held fresh toast, butter, two kinds of jam, a plate of scrambled eggs, a bowl of Greek yogurt with fresh fruit and, on a separate plate, slices of honeydew melon.

Parker had just finished pouring his coffee when there was a light knocking at the door.

Nick half rose, alarmed. Who the fuck was knocking at her door at 7:30 in the morning?

Parker pushed gently on his shoulder. "Down boy," she murmured. "It's not terrorists at the door. It's a pleasant surprise."

She went to the door, opened it and picked something up from the floor. Nick frowned. A plate wrapped in a rectangle of cloth, the four corners of the cloth tied in a knot.

She placed it on the table, unwrapped it and ohmygod.

It was a yellow cake with baked lemon slices on top and it smelled divine.

"Mrs. Da Costa," Parker said, smiling. "I told you she was generous with her baked goods. This is a thank you for carrying her groceries up. Here." A thick wedge landed on his plate and the smell was even more incredible when it was right under his nose. A much smaller slice landed on her plate. "Lemon cake. Her specialty."

Nick speared a chunk with his fork and closed his eyes.

"Good, right?" Parker smiled.

It was moist, not too sweet, very lemony. Perfect.

Nick took a sip from his cup. Perfect coffee.

He looked at the table, with pretty plates filled with luscious food, then looked at Parker, sitting across from him. Smiling at him.

Perfect.

"How is it that every experience I've had with you is a peak experience?"

He hadn't meant it suggestively, but Parker turned stoplight red. When she blushed, she was outlandishly beautiful, and Nick realized that subconsciously he'd included the sex. It had been amazing.

Everything was amazing.

"That, too," he said easily. "But also the food and setting." He put another bite of Mrs. Da Costa's lemon cake in his mouth and sighed. Perfect.

Parker smiled at him. "Wait until today is over. A long day under the sun at an archeological site watching me take notes will not be a peak experience."

Actually, that sounded great.

"We'll see. I promise I won't be bored. And anyway, tonight you're going to cook for me."

"Yep. A promise is a promise."

He suddenly thought of something. "Wait. You're going to spend a long day working. You don't need to cook for me. You'll be tired. We could—"

She held up a hand. "Stop. First of all, I'll owe you." She lay a long slender finger across his mouth when he began to protest. "And believe it or not, cooking relaxes me. And I'd infinitely rather prepare something simple and relax in my own home than go out after a long day. Here. Have some of my raspberry jam. It's baked."

Beneath that lovely exterior was pure steel and Nick understood he wasn't going to get her to change her mind. So he ate her jam on a thick slice of sourdough bread instead. It was perfect.

They ate quietly. Nick tried not to be a pig, but everything was really good, and he'd worked up an appetite. The lemon cake was to die for.

He swallowed and asked the burning question. "Does Mrs. Da Costa's cooking run to tiramisu?" His favorite dessert.

Parker shook her head, shiny hair brushing her shoulders. "Sadly, I think not. I've had the full repertoire, but so far, no tiramisu. I have some tiramisu in the freezer, though. I'll pull it out for dinner this evening."

Nick paused, last forkful halfway to his mouth. "You have tiramisu?"

She nodded. "I do."

"Homemade?"

She was fighting a smile. "It is."

"By *you*?" *Nail it down*, he thought.

"Indeed."

Nick slapped a hand over his chest, somewhere near his heart. "Oh God. You can make tiramisu. Marry me."

Parker laughed. "You're so easy. A dessert and you're already proposing?"

He nodded. "Tiramisu is one of my weaknesses. Now that I've found a source, I'm going to guard it. Like a dragon hoards its treasure."

"Well, Smaug. I only have three bowls of it. I hope that will be enough. I'll give you mine. Three portions."

"No way." Nick frowned. "I can't take your portion."

"No, you can have it. I can always make more, just not today. And you'll earn the extra portion because you're going to have a long, hot, boring day."

A day spent with Parker. "It might be long and hot, but it definitely won't be boring."

Silence. They looked at each other. There were things being said silently. Nick didn't catch it all—women were better at that—but he caught enough.

Yeah. Something was definitely happening.

Parker rose, dishes in hand. "We should get going. We'll have to stop by your hotel. You can't be out on a dig in that elegant outfit fit for *Il Terrazzone*. I'm hoping you packed for roughing it."

Nick rose, too. "I did. I always pack for the possibility

of going on a hike. Though these past few years, where I was, going hiking was taking your life in your hands. Here, let me help you."

The two of them cleared the table quickly and Parker loaded the dishwasher.

Parker picked up a tablet and a laptop and put them into a backpack and bent to pick up a cooler. "I made a picnic lunch for us. I hope you like tuna fish sandwiches. I also made ham and cheese."

"They'll be great," Nick said as he took the cooler from her hands. "And thanks."

She frowned up at him. "You're dedicating a day to me, probably two or three, and you're thanking me for making a few sandwiches? The least I could do."

They were at the door. "Stop thanking me. I'm delighted to trail along. But it's going to be fiercely hot. You're going to need a—"

"Hat," she said, and pulled out a wide brimmed hat from a tote bag near the door.

Nick ran a finger down her cheek. The skin was soft. He knew how soft she was all over. "And make sure you have sunscreen. If you don't, we can stop somewhere on the way."

She pulled out a yellow tube from the bag. He could see 50 SPF on it. "Already there, mom. No worries. Sheesh."

"Don't want this skin to get burned."

Any other woman would have bristled, but she just smiled at him.

"We ready?"

"I guess we are. I'll be fast at my hotel. I want to be on the road before rush hour. When's rush hour?"

Parker locked the door and sighed. "Always. Traffic is always bad. But it's particularly bad from around nine to ten."

"We'll beat the traffic."

Nick made it to his hotel along the Bay in record time. They walked into the immense lobby, and he felt a secret thrill walking in, Parker on his arm. He'd left yesterday evening, a boring businessman, and was walking back in with a prize on his arm.

The hotel lobby was spectacular. Sleek and modern without being soulless.

"Do you want to come up or do you want to wait for me in the lobby?"

She looked around. "I've never been here. It's really nice. I think I'll wait for you here."

Nick sat her down in one of the numerous elegant conversation sets. Behind her chair was an explosion of bouquets and she looked like a queen.

"Good call. I'll be fast." On his way to the bank of elevators, Nick ordered a cappuccino for her.

In the room he changed into cargo pants, a light long-sleeved shirt, boots and a ball cap. He also packed a go bag with several changes of clothes, his shaver, toothbrush and toiletries. Some gear he always had with him. And a box of condoms.

God yes.

Jesus, he couldn't wait to get back down to her.

She was sipping her cappuccino, reading the hotel copy of an Italian newspaper, *La Repubblica*.

"Hey."

She smiled at him. "Hey yourself. Thanks for the cappuccino."

He shrugged, passed a hand over her hair. "Everything okay with the world?"

Usually, Nick was always super plugged in. He subscribed to a lot of online newspapers and political newsletters and a couple of databases and usually checked hourly. He hadn't checked any source of news in over fourteen hours.

Parker sighed. "Not really. There's a low-level war just started in the Republic of Congo, an earthquake in Tibet, a new viral outbreak of a mystery disease in Shanghai and the Pope's in the hospital again."

He already had men in Congo. Nothing he could do about Tibet or Shanghai. "Sorry to hear that. He's a good man."

"He is. Are we ready?"

"Yeah." Nick reached down to give her a hand. She didn't need a hand getting out of the armchair, but he liked touching her. He kept her hand in his and tucked it into his arm and walked out of his hotel with the most beautiful woman in Naples on his arm.

CHAPTER
Seven

Oh man, having a personal driver—a really good personal driver—who also carried your bags for you and, incidentally, was a sex god, was definitely the way to go.

Instead of making the trip in a sweat of anxiety because there were few signposts and dozens of backroads to take, and it was so easy to get lost, Parker was whisked in enormous comfort directly there. Somehow, Nick navigated his way unerringly to the archeological park with only GPS coordinates and that weird male sense of direction she hadn't been blessed with.

And she'd been able to catch up with her email. It had taken an hour to get there—traffic was hellish—and she read with increasing fascination something her little group of nerds in Oxford had found.

The vehicle had stopped, and Parker pulled herself out of her study trance.

"End of the line," Nick announced.

"What?" She lifted her head and looked around. They were at the entrance of the park. "We're not there. The villa is still two and a half kilometers away."

"We're as far as we can go without busting our way in. And the guard isn't here." Nick pointed at the barrier across the road into the site.

"*What?*" Parker was fully oriented now. "It's past ten. Matteo is supposed to be in the guardhouse by eight. He's either an hour late or he's off having a second breakfast."

Nick turned his head, frowning. "That's the security at this place? One guy who scampers off?"

Parker sighed. "Pretty much."

Nick took in the view. This part of the Campi Flegrei was flat and as far as the eye could see there wasn't much except for the odd pile of rocks denoting a dig. Most of what was interesting was underground.

There wasn't much of anything. Certainly no people.

It had been creepy as hell working here two days ago. Parker could finally admit to herself that truth.

"I'm glad you're here," she said quietly.

"I'm glad I'm here," he replied. "How do we get in if the guard has gone to Naples to get his coffee?"

"Magic trick." Parker reached into the side of her backpack and pulled out a remote control. The guard had been gone the last time she'd been here, too. Luckily, she'd been assigned the remote. She clicked and the long arm barring the entrance creaked and started lifting slowly.

"That's not a steel barrier," Nick said angrily. "It's

wood. This car could crash through it without scratching the hood. Anyone could get through it."

She sighed. It was true.

"Drive down this main road for a kilometer and a half and turn right where it says *SCAVI*. Excavations."

The road was rutted but Nick somehow managed to make the ride as smooth as possible. When she'd gone down it in her Smartcar, it had nearly rattled her teeth out of her head.

"You were really engrossed in what you were reading." Nick was driving slowly and carefully.

"Yeah." Parker shot a glance at him. "Sorry about that. I wasn't very good company."

He shook his head. "No. Didn't mean that at all. It's just that you looked absorbed. Good news?"

"The best, actually." Parker smiled. "Do you remember I told you about a group of baby nerds I had working for me in Oxford? Going through archives?"

"Yes." Nick looked over at her, face serious. "I remember every word you've ever said to me."

Oh. The words, spoken in his deep voice, hit a chord. It took her breath away for a moment.

"Well, my nerdlings found a possible correspondence between the owner of the villa we're going to study and a friend of his who was stationed in Britannia. The owner of the villa, Lucius Varrus, quit Rome under Caligula, frightened of the emperor's craziness, though of course he couldn't say that. He came close, though, in what he obviously thought was a private correspondence. He was clear that he wanted out of Rome in the worst way and that he thought Caligula was going to burn Rome to the ground. As it happened, that was Nero. Oh! Turn right here—"

But Nick was already turning.

"Caligula. Wasn't he the guy who elected a horse to the Senate? Though I've met some senators and a good horse would definitely be better. Smarter. Saner."

"He threatened to make his horse a consul, yes. And he declared war on the sea. Lots of craziness. No wonder Lucius Varrus, if he's our guy, wanted out." She pointed out the window. "See that outcropping with the shed? That's our spot."

Nick drove them to the spot and parked.

They sat for a moment in silence, listening to the ticking of the cooling engine.

Parker reached out and covered Nick's hand on the wheel with her own. "Thanks so much for driving us. I was in a sweat of anxiety the whole way when I did it. You made it seem like a walk in the park."

Nick moved his hand and clasped hers, bringing it to his mouth. He kissed the back of her hand. "It was nothing."

"Not nothing." Parker shook her head. "And now you have a whole day of waiting around watching me taking photos and notes. It's not going to be fun."

"Wouldn't be in any other place in the world."

Nick was being really nice, but she knew what he was in for. Immense tedium, in blazing heat.

Well, he was a big boy. If he didn't want to be here, he wouldn't be.

He helped her down, though she had on trousers and could have managed on her own. But it was really nice to be helped down. It was really nice having been driven here. It was really nice having someone carry her gear.

She remembered a friend in college who dated a guy her friends just didn't get. He was incredibly boring...but super reliable. When her friends asked why him, she said life was easier with four hands instead of two.

Life *was* easier with Nick. Last time she'd been here, she'd arrived stressed because the traffic was its usual hellish Neapolitan self. She'd had to wrangle her gear out of the car and lug it around, never able to leave it because she had expensive gear that was very attractive to thieves.

She did not have to worry about thieves with Nikolai Garin looking after her stuff.

The villa was surrounded by scaffolding, with a small steel corrugated hut, its door secured by a padlock.

"So," Parker said with a wave of her hand at the square excavation. "Voilà."

Nick stowed her gear neatly and looked with interest at what, at first view, was a big hole in the ground. "Roman villa, huh?"

She smiled at him. "Two thousand years have added about twenty feet of material to the site. At the bottom is the street level in Roman times. We think it was a villa that was also fortified. That was the entrance." She cocked her head as she looked at the dig. "Do forts always face the same way?"

"No." Nick started walking the perimeter and she walked with him. "A fortification always uses surrounding geography, the shape of the site. If there is a hill or raised rocky outcropping, that will be used as one of the walls. Rivers and forests can be used as defense mechanisms."

"All of southern Italy was covered in forests which were cut down. There was probably a forest or at least woods nearby. Though wood wasn't used much in construction. The Romans used stone."

Nick nodded. "Smart. Are you going in? I don't see any stairs. And I don't have any rope with me."

Parker smiled. "I don't have any rope with me either. But I do have something else."

They'd walked around the site and were back at the hut. Parker opened the door with her key and waited for her eyes to adjust.

Inside was shelving holding the tools of the archeologists' trade—shovels and brushes and sifters. And a ladder.

"Let me." Nick picked up the ladder and placed it into the excavation. "I'll go down first," he said and waited. He wanted her approval.

"Okay," she said. He wanted to go down first? Fine. The ladder wasn't rickety, but it did rest against friable soil.

"You're going to need your gear." His raised eyebrows made it a question.

"Yes. I can get it later."

"I'll get it." And he did. Two satchels, the cooler and a

bag were heavy and bulky, but he went down that ladder smooth as cream. She'd had to awkwardly wrangle her way down and it had taken three trips.

She went down smoothly too, since she wasn't carrying anything, and smiled up at him. "Am I glad you're here. You're making everything easier for me. Thanks."

He waited a beat then ran a long forefinger down the side of her face. He'd done that last night, too, only while he was inside her. The memory of that made her thighs clench.

God, she'd thought herself almost asexual, but she wasn't. She wasn't at all.

"Happy to do it," he said, his voice low. "Happy to be here."

They stood for a moment inside the hole in the ground that hid a Roman villa, in the shade of a frescoed wall. Everything was in sharp focus for Parker. The bright late morning sun outlined the rocks and low brick walls and remnants of frescoes. The villa smelled of earth and the plants growing out of the walls. They were standing where humans had stood two thousand years ago. Maybe just like this? A man and a woman facing each other, far from home.

The extra focus was all Nick. Clearly, hormonal over-load kicked something into gear. It was a good something, and useful, and she planned on using it to the fullest.

She smiled up at him. "Right. You going to be okay? I'm going to take photos and videos and dictate notes." She pointed to a doorway with wooden lintels. "I'll be going through that door, there are several other rooms. Don't freak if you don't see me. I can hear you if you call out. Please don't touch anything, including the dirt walls. That's Roman dirt, two thousand years old."

There. She'd covered various possibilities.

"Will you be ok?" Parker was still worried he'd be bored.

As an answer, Nick sat on the ground and pulled from his backpack a ruggedized tablet that looked like it could withstand gunfire and settled against the ladder, not touching anything.

He switched on the tablet, gave a thumbs up and grinned at her. "I've got three contracts to go over and some after-action reports to study. I'll be fine. Call me if you need anything."

He looked settled and content. He was doing his thing. Okay. That meant that Parker could do her thing. She disappeared into her head and into the Roman villa and slid back two thousand years. As she walked around, drinking in the shape of the villa, with what must have been a garden with a fountain at its center, the book began to take shape in her head.

It was always an exciting moment when a thousand factoids began to coalesce, when she could start to *see* the book. And maybe the documentary. An incredible feeling.

In the back of her mind, she was aware that this fast coming together of a thesis, of the heart of the book, was also thanks to the blond giant sitting quietly in the main room of the villa. She'd left him scrolling through his oversized tablet, engrossed, but she had no doubt that if there were a problem, he'd snap into action. A mantle of protection had been spread over her, allowing her to sink into the project. She didn't have to pay attention to the outside world because he was doing it for her.

She was so steeped in Roman culture that she could feel, could almost *see* the life of Lucius Varrus. The rhythms of it, the seasons. From the documentation she and her nerdlings had been able to gather, Lucius Varrus never went back to Rome. He lived during the reign of Caligula, and it was a period marked by the dangers of having an insane man with vast powers rule over you.

They hadn't mapped out the entire villa yet, but initial ground radar showed room after room after room, with small structures adjacent to the villa. If she interpreted the situation correctly, Varrus owned a vast landholding and would be, in many ways, self-sufficient. Self-sufficient in food and water. The Roman empire was still peaceful, and he wouldn't have to worry about thieves or bandits. He would have had a pleasant life. Subject to taxation, of course, but far enough outside the immediate reach of Rome to fashion for himself an independent existence. The household, comprising immediate and extended family, a farm manager and his family, and a number of slaves, would have been large. Over a hundred people.

She walked around, taking hundreds of photos and videos and dictating her thoughts into the recording app of her phone.

It was really coming together.

Just as she was dictating her thoughts about food self-sufficiency, her stomach rumbled, and she checked the time. Past noon. Time for lunch. They'd had a nice breakfast but then they'd burned a ton of calories in the night.

As she walked into the frescoed room where she'd left Nick, he looked up. Their eyes met. It was like a punch to the stomach, but a nice one.

"You up for lunch?" she asked.

He smiled. "God yeah."

And she realized he was hungry, but that he wouldn't have said anything until she wanted to eat. Luckily, she'd packed a really nice lunch.

Parker sat down next to Nick, cross-legged, and pulled the cooler over. "Let it not be said that I put you to work and didn't feed you."

His eyes lit up. "God forbid."

"Okay, we're starting with sandwiches. Tuna and ham and cheese. Which do you want first?"

"Tuna."

"Here you go." She handed over a jumbo tuna sandwich with a smile. She was really proud of her tuna sandwiches. Thick slices of fresh sourdough bread, lightly toasted, lots of creamy tuna salad. The sandwich was over an inch thick.

Nick took a big bite and his eyes widened. He swallowed. "Whoa."

She took a bite of her own. Yeah, it was good.

Nick bent his head over the cooler. "What else you got in here?"

"Let's see... Ham and cheese sandwiches, chunks of parmesan cheese with apple slices, a container with a tomato and mozzarella salad, another container with a big slice of eggplant parmesan, two slices of Mrs. Da Costa's lemon cake, one extra-large and one normal, and some grapes." Enough even for the appetite of a big guy. "Oh, and drinks." She pulled out two large thermoses, took two tin cups and poured the contents of one in. "Here. You must be thirsty. The second thermos is water."

He chugged the tin cup and shook his head. "Wow. Freshly squeezed orange juice and...?"

"Lemon and honey."

He polished everything off quickly and neatly, scrupulously eating only his half and making sure she ate. It was past noon and hot, and her appetite disappeared in the heat. After half a tuna sandwich, a couple of bites of eggplant parmesan and fruit, she was done, insisting that Nick continue. After offering her food a billion times, he finally understood she didn't want any more and finished everything off, down to the last crumbs of Mrs. Da Costa's lemon cake.

Parker finished half an hour before him and watched him eat, pleased. He loved everything. "Man," he said finally, leaning back against the ladder. "That's the second-best meal I've had in years."

Parker smiled. "It was just a picnic lunch."

Nick shook his head. "It was pure ambrosia of the gods. Everything is perfect. The only thing missing was tiramisu but—" he shot her a sly look. "You're going to feed me tiramisu tonight, right?"

"Count on it. Three bowls full if you can manage. Creamy and chocolatey."

He sighed and slapped a hand on his chest. He rolled his head toward her and smiled. "You've *got* to marry me."

Parker laughed. "Over tiramisu? Like I said before, you're selling yourself cheaply."

He scowled. "Cheap? You're calling me cheap? I'll have you know…" Dust bounced on the ground in a strange dance. Nick stopped suddenly, then threw himself over her.

And the world ended.

CHAPTER

Eight

It was pitch black, the world gone in darkness. Parker couldn't see anything. She couldn't breathe. She tried to pull air in her lungs but something heavy was over her, crushing her and she couldn't *breathe!*

Parker coughed. Her lungs were filled with dust, and she had to cough to free them. Coughing hurt. Something incredibly heavy was on top of her and something wet was dripping on her.

Nothing made any sense. Her breaths were shallow, rasping—each inhale a struggle through a throat clogged with grit. The air around her was heavy, claustrophobic, thick with the dry sting of pulverized stone.

And the boulder on her back made it almost impossible to breathe. Parker tried to take stock. Something was holding her down from her head to her feet, and she couldn't move. She tried expanding her lungs against the boulder and...the boulder moved! It shifted and she could feel a faint rhythmic beat against her back as if the stone had a heart that was beating.

Awareness rushed in and she realized she was buried underground. That last moment blossomed in her mind. Laughing with Nick, and then the dust on the ground suddenly dancing, and then Nick throwing himself over her.

An earthquake. A huge one. They were buried alive inside the Roman villa. The utter darkness was suddenly intolerable, suffocating. She moved her right arm with difficulty down her side to her pants and yes! The outline of her cell. She extracted it with difficulty.

The boulder on top of her was Nick.

"Nick!" Parker cried. "Are you okay?"

There was no answer, only a long, deep groan.

Parker brought the cell up to her face and switched it on. Light! Her home screen was a photo of the bay at noon, and it was full of light. She held the cell out and tried to turn her head to see Nick, but she didn't have any range of movement. His heavy body covered hers completely and now she saw that he was buried in rubble. Heavy stones and bricks on his back, as far up as she could see in the dim light.

She switched to flashlight mode and held the cell up to his face, turning as much as she could.

"Jesus," she whispered.

He was covered in blood. There was an open gash along his hairline that was still dripping blood. His arm, too, was covered in gashes that were bleeding. His shoulder was wounded. He'd taken the hit, and she was unharmed. She was under the weight of his body, but she wasn't cut or bleeding or even in pain anywhere.

Nick throwing himself over her before she even realized there was an earthquake had saved her life.

And endangered his?

The thought of an injured or—God!—dying Nick was terrifying.

She placed the cell in flashlight mode on the dusty ground and moved her arm slowly until she could grasp his shoulder. She shook him, gently at first, then more strongly. His muscles were so thick she couldn't move him. When she pulled her hand away, it was covered in blood.

"Nick! Nick! Can you hear me? Oh God, Nick, answer me!"

He groaned but didn't open his eyes.

"Nick," she pleaded.

Nick's eyelids fluttered. His breathing deepened.

"Come back to me. *Please.*"

She fumbled in her pocket, remembering she had a packet of tissues. It was hard, one-handed, to extract them but she did, pulling out some tissues, pressing them against the side of his head. Carefully, because that gash looked really ugly. The tissue turned red immediately. It took the whole packet, but finally the bleeding slowed to a trickle. Parker had taken a first aid course a billion years ago but remembered nothing in her panic for Nick. But stopping bleeding was definitely a good thing. Something she should be doing.

She angled her phone's light beam so she could see his arm better and winced at the torn flesh. Another big gash that wasn't bleeding so badly but she could see a massive bruise on his shoulder, already swelling. Something had fallen heavily on him. That something would have fallen on her if he hadn't had such fast reflexes and thrown himself over her.

She panned her flashlight around, heart heavy. They were buried in rubble, heavy blocks of stone and brick and dirt. They were buried at least twenty feet underground, if they were at the street level of the Roman villa. Deeper if they'd fallen into a fissure.

They were buried alive. They might die here in this airless tomb of rubble.

No!

Parker refused to die here. Not now. Not when she'd just met the most fascinating man in the world. Not when she was working on a project of the heart. It wasn't her time to die and it definitely wasn't Nick's.

She tried to shake his shoulder and watched his eyelids flutter. Stretching her arm, she slapped his cheek, over and over.

"Nick! Wake up! Come back to me!"

Finally, his eyes half opened, closed, opened again. But there was no recognition in his gaze. Bending herself like a pretzel, Parker held her flashlight up to his face and tried to look into his eyes. She had a partial view, but it didn't seem to her that his pupils were different sizes. Which meant that maybe he wasn't concussed.

Please.

Terror was like a cloud around her, and she needed Nick with her if she had any hope of holding it together. They needed to figure this out together. How to emerge from who knows how many tons of rubble and somehow find their way to the surface. How not to die here, a million miles from anywhere.

No one was coming for them. No one even knew they were here. The gatekeeper hadn't seen them come in and, in any case, would definitely have made a beeline for his home in an earthquake without a second thought. The gateway wasn't sophisticated and didn't register who passed through with the remote control.

The Superintendency had given her permission to spend time at the site, but there had been no discussion of when. They wouldn't assume she was here and—she admitted to herself—wouldn't come looking for her.

No one would be looking for her.

This had been a big one. There would be chaos everywhere. Even Aunt Caroline would take a while to wonder where she was, maybe days, because the Consulate definitely took precedence over an honorary niece.

She and Nick had to get out of here under their own steam and Nick had to be conscious because Parker couldn't drag him. And she wouldn't leave him.

"Nick!" Parker made her voice sharp. A fall of dust trickled down. Parker lowered her voice. "Nick! Come back!" She pushed against his shoulder, hoping she was avoiding his wound.

Nick's eyes opened, closed. Opened. He frowned. "Parker?"

"Yes! Thank God."

"Are you okay?"

"I'm fine, Nick. You saved me. But you have a head wound and you shoulder is banged up."

His head lifted slightly, and though she could tell it hurt him, he didn't make a sound.

"Where are we exactly? Can you tell?"

It hadn't even occurred to her to try to tell where they were. The earthquake could have tossed them anywhere. She directed the flashlight cell along the floor which was mostly broken shards and sand. A couple of feet away, a section of corrugated steel siding from the above-ground hut had fallen in a way as to provide shelter, like a lean to. Parker scrabbled with her hand, bringing things close to her face. She brought a fistful of reddish sand, shards of terracotta and...yes! Two broken pieces of stucco. Painted bright blue.

"We're still in the Blue Room where we were having lunch, right up against the wall. But I think it has imploded." She tried again to expand her ribs to get a full lungful of air. "Nick, we need to move, see if we can find a way out. But I don't know how because you've got rubble on top of you."

He didn't answer. She twisted to see his face and panicked. His eyes were closed again. "Nick!"

His eyes popped open, and Parker shone her cell's light

on them, letting out a relieved breath. His pupils still looked to be the same size.

A huge hand landed next to her shoulder, lifting a small cloud of dust. Startled, Parker angled her head to look at his face.

"We have to get out from under this rubble," Nick said. His face was streaked with blood and what she could see of his face was ashen. He was in great pain but sounded cogent.

He was back.

Parker let out her breath. Trying to figure out a way to save them without Nick's help, with an unconscious Nick...well, she couldn't do it. She'd been close to losing it. Being in the dark under who knew how much rubble—it was a nightmare, and she was holding on to her sanity by a thread. But Nick's matter of fact tone reassured her.

The alternative... Her phone had a seventy-five percent charge, but if she kept it on flashlight mode it wouldn't last much more than an hour. She had a recharger, but it was in the vehicle and might as well have been on the dark side of the moon for all the good it did her there. Who knew if the vehicle had even survived the earthquake?

Parker suffered from mild claustrophobia, and one side effect was fear of the dark. When the phone went out, they would be in utter darkness, buried under tons of rubble, no one coming for them. And if Nick was out cold... She had to stop herself from hyperventilating.

"Nick?" Parker's voice quavered and she had to stop, breathe deeply. "Nick, what do we do?"

She saw Nick look carefully around and realized it was the first time he consciously took in what had happened. He didn't change expression, wasn't panicking, and she felt her own panic subside a little. He met her eyes, and she saw no fear and her panic dissipated a little more.

"This panel has created a void. We need to move into it. We need to get out from the rubble."

She blinked. That made sense. They couldn't do anything as long as they were pinned down.

"How? What do we do?"

Her neck ached from trying to twist to see his face. But his face was what was keeping her sane. An anchor of sanity in a world gone crazy.

"Ok. I'm going to try to lift myself up and you try to slide out from under me."

Wait. He was talking about her sliding out, not him. Parker saw exactly what he was doing. Sacrificing himself. Making sure she made it by taking the weight of the rubble onto himself.

"No."

She saw him blink. "No?" He sounded dumbfounded. Clearly trying to wrap his head around someone saying no to him.

"No. We're both going to get out of this or neither of us will."

"Parker, if you don't get out, you will die here."

"And so will you. So, we're getting out together."

Parker still felt fuzzy, not quite herself, but she was sure of this. They were in terrible trouble, but they'd face it together. She needed him but he also needed her. "So figure something out, fast."

Silence. Slowly, Nick's arms embraced her in a tight hold. His legs encased and held hers.

"Okay, this is what is going to happen. I'm going to see if I can press upward as hard as I can. With luck I can buy us a second or two in which we'll have more freedom of movement. The rubble is interlocking and if I manage to shift the big pieces, it will take them a little time to settle back. All we need is a second or two." He tightened his hold on her, using his arms and legs. "The instant we have room for maneuver, I'm going to roll us toward that piece of siding. Got it?"

She envisioned it for a moment, which is something she always did before doing something hard, running it through in her mind's eye until she could see what was going to happen.

"Got it. We roll fast once you've shifted the weight upwards."

"Yeah."

Parker didn't mention the fact that it would be almost impossible for Nick to shift all that weight bearing down on them. She had no way to assess how deep the rubble was, how heavy. Nick was strong but this seemed impossible. Not to mention the fact that he was wounded, had lost blood.

But what choice was there? If they stayed here, pinned

down, unable to move, they'd die. If his attempt was unsuccessful and just managed to bring more rubble down on them... God. They were done for.

She couldn't show her doubts. He was going to try something basically impossible, requiring strength and courage. If he failed, the bricks would fall on him, but he would be shielding her. She owed him her support.

"What can I do to help?"

"Move with me, the instant I tell you to."

"Okay."

"I'm going to count to three and start pushing up, but don't move until I say so. Yeah?"

"Yeah." They might die. They might survive. It all depended on Nick's strength and the configuration of bricks and shards above them. He could fail. The rubble could bury them even more. But it was the only chance they had.

"One...two...three!"

It was extraordinary. Under him, Parker could feel Nick as he strained against the weight over him. The body above her turned to iron as he pushed up. An immense force, there in the dust, strong as the quake, exerting force upward when the earth itself was bearing down on him.

Nick's shoulders were shaking with the effort when he suddenly arched up, shaking off some rubble to the right and...

"Now!" he grunted, and Parker threw herself to the left, encased in Nick's arms. He rolled them out from the pile as it fell to the ground. Dust rose up and Parker started coughing. Nick turned her around, then sat up with her in his arms. He pounded her back until she managed to get most of the dust out.

She looked around at the small space, lit by her cell, casting dark-edged shadows. What had fallen on them had dropped into a jumble, dark and impenetrable and entrapping them no more. They were at least able to move around a little in the lee of the corrugated steel panel. They couldn't stand up—certainly Nick couldn't—but they could sit up which was infinitely better than lying crushed under an immense weight in the dust, unable to move.

She was held tightly by Nick, and he was the only thing keeping her sane. His strength was her bulwark against panic.

They sat in the dust, holding tightly to each other until Nick put his hands on her shoulders and pulled away. It felt awful not to be held by Nick. "You okay?" he asked.

Which was rich. He was the one who was wounded, who had taken the brunt of the world falling on them.

"Yeah." Parker touched the side of his face where the gash was. It had stopped bleeding. "What about you?"

Nick didn't answer. He'd picked up her cell and shone it around, studying their surroundings intently. There wasn't much to study. Rocks and bricks and dirt. The frightening jumble which was left when the earth moved.

"We have to get out of here," he said and she nodded. He studied the display of her cell. "No coverage. We'll have to get closer to the surface to be able to call for help. I have my satphone with me, but it needs line of sight with the satellites."

"We need to be fast getting out of here," Parker said, worried. "The flashlight function uses the battery up and my recharger is in your vehicle."

"That's ok. When your battery runs out, we'll use my satphone and I have a recharger with me."

She glanced down at his cargo pants, dirty and blood-stained, with a billion pockets. "Hooray for cargo pants."

He smiled at her. It was a crooked smile, with blood-caked dust providing the only spots of color in an ashen face. He was trying to buck her up because he understood as well as she did that they were in terrible trouble.

"Where's the next room?"

"North. But I have no idea where north is."

He bent his head over his complicated watch and pointed to his right. "There. That's north."

"You have a compass in your watch?"

He nodded.

"Then we need to keep heading north. The Blue Room was at the end of a wing. We'll have to keep moving until we find a path through the rubble that will take us up. Without getting crushed in the meantime."

Their eyes met. She knew he knew how almost impossible that was going to be. They were quite possibly already dead, and in their tomb, only they didn't know it yet.

Parker was so grateful she was with Nick. He was probably regretting his offer to accompany her, but she was so glad to have him. She was barely holding it together, but though he was wounded and bloody, Nick looked perfectly capable. Just looking at him calmed her.

Without him, she'd...she'd die. She wouldn't even know where north was. She had zero survival instincts. She'd blunder about until she triggered another fall of material which might crush her. Break bones. She'd keep her cellphone on until the battery ran out because she hated the dark. And then she'd just wait for death in the dark.

Instead, crazily, she thought they might have a chance. Nick was carefully studying their surroundings, and she was sure he'd come up with a plan. It was the way he was wired. He wouldn't give up until they were dead, which might not actually happen.

"What's north, Parker? What's in the rooms along the wing?"

Parker closed her eyes and tried to think. "Not much. No frescoes. The walls aren't stuccoed, they are dirt. The rooms aren't even fully excavated."

"Are they faced with brick?"

Parker tried to focus. The focus of the team had been on the frescoed room, which had soaked up time and attention.

"Not that I recall. Sorry. We were all focused on the Blue Room. The other rooms hadn't been fully excavated, and they were just empty containers."

"That's for the best. If they had had fortified walls, they would have crumbled in the quake. Simple dirt walls

—well, we'd have more luck trying to tunnel through them than pick apart heavy rubble."

Well, that made sense.

"Okay. What do we do now? I mean we have to go north. There's nothing but packed earth to either side."

Nick had finished his careful perusal. "I think I saw an opening." They awkwardly shuffled behind the steel panel. And there it was. Another steel panel in the brick rubble.

Parker studied it. "It's small."

He sighed as he got on hands and knees. "It's what we have."

"Wait." Parker put a hand on his shoulder, feeling strength and determination under her hand. "I think I should try to see how far I can get. I'm smaller than you."

"Absolutely not." Nick scowled. "We don't know if getting in there might not precipitate another collapse. At least here you'll be safe."

"Until the next aftershock." Parker measured the opening with her hands and brought her hands to his chest. Her hands didn't even span two thirds of his chest. No way he could make his way through. "And at any rate, if something happens to you, I'm done for."

Without waiting for an answer, Parker dropped to her hands and knees and

disappeared.

NICK HAD BEEN in tight spots before. His whole career had been in tight spots. But he was always with fellow soldiers—well-trained men who had his back and he had theirs. He didn't worry about them. They were men who knew what to do and how to do it.

Never with a woman he cared about.

It was hell.

He wasn't entirely certain he could keep her safe. And alive. It ate at him.

He'd recognized an earthquake immediately and thrown himself over Parker. A ton of bricks and dirt rained down on him, and he was definitely dinged, but it would have killed Parker.

He couldn't even go there. He'd just met her, had felt his life being turned around. He couldn't lose her. It was absolutely unthinkable that she be in danger.

And here she was, winnowing her way through tons of dirt and rubble, trying to find perhaps a nonexistent way out of here. Being in a hole during a period of earthquakes was dangerous. He should have thought of that. But it had been pleasantly cool in the excavated room, and the frescoes that were visible were incredibly beautiful.

Not much beauty in his life these past years. And now there was Parker and a Roman villa, and the coolness factor had been off the charts. Had he been thinking with his little head?

Not really. If they were going to take a lunch break, it would have had to be in his vehicle with the AC on or sitting out in the dust and heat. Nick opted for lunch in the excavated villa. Parker had worked hard all morning, and he wanted her to relax.

And they'd been having a good time—and he'd eaten his silly head off—until Earth lashed out. He had no idea what this quake had been on the Mercalli scale, but it was much stronger than the one yesterday.

Chances were good they were going to die here. If they didn't find a path up and out, no one was coming to save them. They would die of thirst before they died of hunger, assuming some aftershock didn't bring a boulder down on their heads.

Dying of thirst, encased in a dark tomb, would not be a pleasant way to go.

Nick usually could game his way out of anything. Figure out a way or two to get out of a situation, but this—he was no match for tons of rubble.

He checked his watch. Parker had been gone for a quarter of an hour. It felt like a lifetime. He made a megaphone of his hands. "Parker!" he shouted. "Are you okay?" He turned his head, so his ear was at the small opening she'd wriggled through before disappearing.

"Yes!" Parker's voice carried faintly. No way to tell how far away she was.

Nick tried hard to keep the anxiety out of his voice. He didn't do anxiety, not even in the direst of circumstances, but there it was. He was anxious. He didn't want Parker to die. He'd just found her. He couldn't lose her. She'd opened a door in his head and shown him things he didn't know could be his. She couldn't die. *He* didn't want to die. But he calculated their odds at fifty-fifty, if that.

"I'm ok!"

Was he hallucinating or did her voice sound closer?

He was good at echolocation, like a bat, but her voice would bounce off thousands of angles, be distorted. No way to tell where it came from or even how far away she was. All he could do was wait. If she wanted him to move, she'd tell him.

So Nick knelt in the dirt, eyes fixed on the hole Parker disappeared into. He didn't pull out his own cell. The dark didn't bother him. Darkness was a soldier's friend. He recognized that Parker was afraid of the dark. Lots of people were. She'd had an unsettled childhood, and it was normal that it left her with a fear of not being able to tell what was around her.

Parker, Parker, Parker he thought. Come back to me.

PARKER CRAWLED THROUGH THE OPENING, barely managing to squeeze her way forward and avoiding a jagged piece of metal. No way could Nick make his way through. He'd cut himself to ribbons.

Moving slowly, feeling her heart beat against her ribs, expecting a cascade of rocks and dirt to fall on her at every moment, she wriggled forward. Somehow, every time she came to an impasse, there was an opening, all she had to do was find it. She crawled forward in the dirt and dust, inch by inch, careful when she shifted something to make sure it didn't precipitate a collapse of material. She moved forward, came to what must have been the third room, and the cellphone flashlight dimmed a little. Dread rushed

through her. The idea of being caught here without light...
It messed with her head. Finally, she reached a point
where she could stand up. Sort of. Nick would be bent
over but at least he wouldn't have to be on his hands and
knees.

There was something in the air... She held her hand
up. The air was moving! Very faint, but there. Cool air,
smelling of must. Aiming her cell at a wall of material, she
saw an irregular hole. Putting her hand in front of it, she
felt cool air. Moving. There was enough of an opening for
her to stick her hand in. Parker hesitated for a moment,
remembering every horror movie she'd ever seen where
someone stuck their hand into a hole filled with scorpions
or spiders. Or snakes.

She pushed her hand through the hole and felt cool
moist air and a faint breeze.

She shivered and angled her cell so it would shine into
the hole. Somehow, the darkness was not absolute. There
was a little light coming from up top. She tried to shine the
light up but couldn't see anything.

It was mainly empty space. She tried to look deeper
but couldn't. But clearly there was some kind of structure
that held. And a little light, which meant that there was an
opening to the outside world.

"Parker!"

She lifted her head at the sound of Nick's deep voice.
It was dulled, sounded far away. But he was calling her.

"Here!" she called out.

"Are you okay?"

"Yes!"

A fall of dust trickled between stones. No yelling. Instead of screaming out a message, she started crawling her way back.

On the way she pulled out a stone, a brick, a piece of wood, shifted a fall of dirt, to make the passage larger. Eliminated anything that might cut him. Faster than expected, she was back to where they started, under the steel panel.

She stuck her hand through the opening and Nick grasped it, helping her through.

Nick grasped her shoulders. "Are you all right? Where did you go?"

Where did she go? She had no idea. All she knew was that it was away from here, and away from here was good.

"I found a sort of path away from here. It leads to what I think is an opening. It's tight though."

"And you came back? Why didn't you break out?"

Parker's eyes widened. She couldn't believe he said that and scowled at him. "Nikolai Garin! Is that what you think of me? That I would find a way out and just...leave you? I can't believe you'd think that! What's the matter with you? Would you leave me?"

His eyes fell to the dirt floor. "No," he confessed.

"Remind me to be really angry with you later. For now, let's see if I have actually found a way out. Getting there and coming back I widened the path as much as I could."

"Can I make it through?"

"I tried to clear it some. Open it up." She tried smiling,

though it cost her. She was still mad at him. "I am really good at Jenga."

She got down on hands and knees. "I'll go first. I hope I remember the way. If you get stuck, I'll try to pull away some more rubble and hope I don't bring the whole thing down on top of us."

"Okay." Nick's face was grim, covered in blood and dirt. It was clear he was unhappy at having her go ahead, but it was the only way. He was extremely chivalrous, but he wasn't stupid. She had to go ahead. She already knew the way and was smaller.

The going was slow and difficult. It was hard to remember the way in the ever-dimming light of her cell. She'd cleared the way as best she could getting back to Nick and continued trying to clear a path. Once she carefully dislodged a stone and got a stream of dirt and stopped. But the way was too narrow for Nick; she tried again, slowly and carefully, and was able to pick apart a jumble to clear room for him.

Every once in a while, she looked back at Nick following her. Once, she winced when she saw him barely make his way through an opening, a section of brick bearing down on the gash in his shoulder. But he didn't make a sound.

Ah! Parker recognized a section she'd come through and had been able to make wider. Nick could get through here easily. And they were close! The air felt a little cooler and was moving.

She had to bend low to get though a slight passageway

and pulled a section of wood away. Miraculously, it didn't start an avalanche. She waited for Nick to clear the section, then turned around in the small space. Nick looked awful. He must have been in pain and was white under his tan. He looked like a monster in a horror movie, caked in dirt and blood. She placed her hand on his shoulder, careful of the deep gash.

"We're close to what I think might be a way out. The air moves, so it must be connected to the outside world, and I think there's a little bit of light. You doing okay?"

"Am I doing—whoa!" Nick suddenly grinned, flakes of crusted blood falling off his cheek. "You're rescuing *me!*"

Parker grinned back. "I am!"

"I'm never going to live this down."

"If we survive," she reminded him, and the grin disappeared.

"We're going to survive," Nick said. He touched her cheek. "I promise."

It was ridiculous. Nick couldn't promise anything of the kind. But she felt better. He was reassurance itself. Tall and broad, radiating strength, even wounded and bleeding. She carefully turned back around, not touching anything. The last thing they needed was another massive spill.

There was a hole in the dirt wall in front of her, and she stuck her hand through again. Cooler air. Air that moved.

Parker stepped back and studied the wall in the feeble light of her dying cell's flashlight. It appeared to be all dirt. Parts of it, at least, didn't seem to be thick. They could possibly scrabble and punch their way through it. She pushed at the borders of the hole and dirt dribbled down.

"I wish I had a pickaxe," Parker said, hands up against the wall, moving them around, looking for weaker spots.

"Don't have a pickaxe, but I do have this," Nick announced, pulling something out of his cargo pants. He opened it up. A knife! Made of some weird substance that wasn't shiny. It was black and looked like it had time-traveled from the future.

"A knife." Parker reached out but Nick held it out of her reach. "Careful honey, it's really sharp."

Parker patted the wall. "We don't need sharp, but we do need strong. Resistant."

"It's strong. Don't worry about that."

Parker frowned at him. "I thought carrying knives was illegal in Italy?"

"Knives over six centimeters. This is five centimeters ninety. And I'd have a special dispensation anyway. Where do I start?"

Parker looked at him, and studied his shoulder. "I think maybe I should start. Then when I find a good spot, you can come in."

Nick was scowling.

"Hold up your left arm," Parker said.

"What?"

"You heard me." He was stalling for time.

Nick brought his left arm up slowly and stopped at chest height. The gash started bleeding.

"Nick," Parker said quietly. "Give the knife to me.

When I've opened something up you can use your other arm."

He winced, but handed it to her, haft first.

Parker patted the wall in a grid. Bottom to top, right to left. The wall felt thin in a few places, but she wasn't able to punch through. The tiny opening she'd originally felt had stones around it.

Her cell was fading fast. She desperately wanted to break through this wall before they were in the dark. She hated darkness, this kind of darkness. Complete and black. It made her think of death.

She tapped a section and felt total horror when her cell died.

"Nick!"

Before she even had time to panic, a bright light came on. Nick's satphone, which had a flashlight like a torch. The area lit up, the light ten times stronger than the light her cell gave off. And he had a charger. They wouldn't be in darkness again for a while.

She let out a long breath.

"Better?" he asked quietly.

"God yeah." She huffed out a breath and said something she'd normally never say, not in a million years. "Not a fan of the dark."

He lifted his good arm to place his hand on her shoulder.

"Not many people are. We have an atavistic fear of the dark. It's in our DNA."

Parker kept patting the wall. She'd been afraid of the

dark since forever. Her boarding schoolteachers had been kind, and she'd always been allowed a night light. She controlled it better, but right now she had to admit to herself that if Nick hadn't had his magic satphone, she'd be freaking.

"I'll bet you're not afraid of the dark."

His hand tightened on her shoulder and fell away. "No, it's trained out of us. We love the dark because it provides cover. And soldiers are self-selected for certain traits anyway."

She sighed.

"On the other hand, I couldn't do what you do. Not in a million years, not with any amount of training."

"I don't know—" Parker stopped.

He picked up on it immediately. "Yeah? You got something?"

She scratched at a section of wall, and it crumbled. A second later, her hand went through. She circled her hand making the hole larger. Cool air circulated and oh God, it felt good. Air moving must come from the world above them, not like the tomb-like air they'd been breathing, undisturbed for centuries. This air was life.

"Here honey, let me." Nick moved in front of her, and she stepped to the side. Yes, he could do this better. She handed him the knife, and he attacked the wall one-handed. His one arm was better than two of hers, and the wall melted as he slashed. Debris rained down, and the hole kept getting bigger until it was a little smaller than a door.

Nick stabbed the knife into the dirt wall to store it and pulled up his satphone and shone it inside the big hole he'd created.

Nick moved his phone around and she could see some kind of circular structure. Definitely modern cement, definitely not Roman. Like some huge tube or pipe. The bottom was round and filled with dirt. She looked up when Nick illuminated the top. There was a huge crack in the cement and some light filtered through. Daylight!

Daylight was salvation! She was moving forward when Nick's good arm barred the way.

"Let me go first. We don't know how fragile this structure is. I don't want a ton of material to fall down on you."

A ton of material had already fallen down on him and wounded him. But Parker knew it was pointless protesting. She stepped aside and Nick moved slowly and warily into the huge hole that had been opened.

He was careful with each step he took, shining his satphone to the roof of the structure about twelve feet high and then back to the flooring. Just when he was about to disappear around a corner he stopped and looked back at her. "Come on. Be careful, but it feels solid. We're in some kind of concrete tunnel that cracked open with the earthquake."

Parker stepped gingerly over the stone threshold and into what he called a tunnel. It probably was. Under her boots, the flooring was stable. Concrete. Who knew how long it had been since the big earthquake, but long enough to get used to unstable surroundings.

The tunnel felt solid. She walked slowly toward Nick. Unafraid that debris would fall on her. Looking up, she could see big cracks in the ceiling where the earthquake had wrenched the tunnel apart. The light she could see through the wide cracks was golden, late afternoon sunlight.

The crack was wide in some areas, big chunks of fallen concrete right underneath. She skirted several on her way to Nick. So grateful to see him by the light of day and not by the light of his satphone. Though they would definitely need the phone when night fell, in a couple of hours.

She looked up uneasily. The top of the tunnel with its cracks was at least twelve feet high. There were points where, with some luck, and if she stood on Nick's shoulders, Parker could perhaps reach the roof. She didn't think she had the upper body strength to pull herself out. Nick had the strength, but he couldn't pull himself out. Not with that wounded shoulder.

She walked straight into Nick's arms and felt them tighten around her. "We're going to make it," he said in his deep voice. Parker mumbled something into his shoulder. They might make it. They might not. If anyone could get them out, it was Nick, but there were no guarantees.

But ohmygod, it felt so good being held by him.

Parker stepped out of his arms. Being held by him was almost addictive. She felt immediately better when she was touching him. But she had to let go because they weren't safe yet.

"Let's follow this tunnel," Nick said and she nodded.

The further away they got from what had almost been their tomb, the better.

They turned the corner and saw a long stretch of tunnel before them. The good news was that the top was even more broken, with long stretches open to the air. The bad news was that there was more rubble to avoid.

Parker looked up. There was a long fissure that opened up enough to accommodate even Nick, though she had no idea how Nick could get up there. "Should we try to get out here?"

"There's a door at the end of this stretch of corridor. Let's see if it leads to an exit."

"There *is?*" Parker squinted as Nick held his satphone up and shone it down the corridor. Yes, there did appear to be a something in the distance. She hadn't noticed it. Hadn't even thought of looking further down. They definitely needed to go look and see what it was. Something was better than nothing.

They walked for what felt like a long time, stepping over concrete rubble. Checking the ceiling constantly. Parker paid attention to what she felt below her feet. At the first sign of shaking she was going to hug the wall. Or hug Nick, whichever was closest.

The ground was dusty and dry and filled with debris. Finally, they came to a halt at the end of the long tunnel.

It was a portal. Or hatch. Or something.

It was huge, round, with that steering wheel-like thing in the center. Like submarines had at the hatches. Made of steel. Completely impenetrable, except that the earthquake had cracked the casing around the big wheel and cracked the circumference.

Nick had suddenly become quiet. Parker looked at him curiously. His face had hardened. Was he seeing something she wasn't?

He pulled at the portal, and it yawned open easily, coming away from one of the two hinges. Nick stepped through and she followed, warily.

At first, Parker had trouble recognizing what she was seeing. Cases, boxes, canisters. It was some kind of deposit? A huge kind of warehouse, so large the end was lost in darkness.

Then she went deeper into the rows and saw that some of the wooden cases were open, and she gasped when she looked inside.

It was a huge weapons cache. Row after row of wooden cases, as far as the eye could see. Many of the cases had been shaken open and she saw rifles spilling out, hundreds and hundreds of them, in pristine condition. Handguns, what looked like thousands upon thousands of them. What must have been rockets, with weird shapes, all aligned along the walls on brackets, many having fallen to the ground. Suitcases with strange electrical gear, not sleek and streamlined, but looking like they came from a movie from the fifties.

Nick was checking the rifles, the suitcases, the guns.

Parker walked around, understanding little of what she saw until she stopped, in horror.

Eight large...things in stainless steel cases. Four long

tubes with a rounded top. Four round metal balls. And next to them, three black curved blades painted against a bright yellow backdrop. The universal sign for...

Parker's hand shot to the mouth. She turned to Nick, horrified.

"Oh my God! Is that—is that..." She pointed with a shaking hand.

"Nuclear weapons," Nick answered grimly. "Yes."

Nine

Nick knew what this was. Bad news. The worst.

Parker knew, too, only her mind rejected it. "Nick?" she whispered, face ashen. "What is this?"

She ran her hand along a tube ending in a bulbous nose cone.

"My guess? It's an arms cache created under Operation Gladio. Do you know what that was?"

"I know what a gladio was. It was the service sword of Roman legionnaires. Short, a stabbing weapon."

"Yeah. The program took its name from the Roman weapon. Operation Gladio was a concerted effort made by NATO and the Italian government to establish arms caches and communications networks in the fifties and early sixties. There was a general feeling that Russia was planning an invasion and was hell bent on conquering Italy, which at the time had the largest Communist party in the West. The idea being that if the Soviets invaded, the resistance could begin right away thanks to these hidden arms caches. But as time went on, apparently some of the locations were lost. But they included more or less everything a resistance would need in terms of arms, explosives, including grenades and mortars, communications equipment, first aid equipment. Including that nuclear warhead you are caressing, called a Davy Crockett."

Parker snatched her hand away from the weapon as if it had turned boiling hot.

She looked around and lowered her voice. "How many nuclear weapons are there?"

Nick had already counted them. "Eight. Four Davy Crocketts and four man portable ones. Those round things over there."

She followed his finger, frowning. They actually didn't look like much, just big round balls of metal. A strong man could, in theory, carry them. Nick certainly could. An atom bomb that a person could carry.

Parker turned around, arms out. "There seems to be enough weaponry and equipment here to start a small war."

Nick nodded. "That's the general idea. The resistance in World War II was still on everyone's mind, and everyone agreed the war would have been won sooner if the resistance had been better armed. So, they decided to arm a possible resistance in advance."

"Were the Soviets really planning on invading Europe?"

"Nobody's clear on that, but there was definitely a

faction in the Soviet military arguing to pour tanks through the Fulda Gap, move down through Germany, over the Alps, and take over Italy. And everyone wanted to be ready if they did."

Parker looked around and he could see that she was starting to appreciate the difficulties, though this wasn't her world.

"What do we do?" she asked quietly.

Good girl. She understood the basics.

"We can't leave these arms unattended. Not with tactical nuclear weapons in the mix. We need to get out or at least get to a place where my satphone is in line of sight with a satellite and call the authorities. And we stay here until a NEST team arrives or at least a team that can defend this arms cache."

"First we call Aunt Caroline, right?"

Nick put his good hand on her arm. "Not first, no. She wouldn't have jurisdiction over nuclear weapons. But we will call her eventually. I don't have the numbers of anyone at the naval base who would be authorized to deal with this. So I'm going to call my partner Jacob Black, who knows everyone and whose name is enough to get attention."

Nick looked up at the ceiling. There were points where he might be able to get through. It would be easy to lift himself through if he didn't have an injured shoulder. But he could definitely push Parker up.

"Listen honey—I don't know what resources there are here in Italy. Don't know if personnel will have to be airlifted from the States. I have to stay here but you sure don't. If I can get you through and if the vehicle wasn't destroyed, you could drive back to Naples. Or call someone to pick you up. I just can't leave until I know this material is in safe hands."

She stiffened and scowled at him. She punched him lightly in the chest, in anger. Ordinarily, he wouldn't even have felt it, but it jolted his shoulder and hurt, a little. He'd have died rather than show it, however.

"Nikolai Garin! There you go again! How dare you assume I'd just up and leave you. And you're *wounded* for God's sake!"

Nick shrugged. It hurt. Fuck. "Just a scratch," he mumbled.

Her eyes bugged and she made a suppressed screaming sound, then stopped and took a deep breath, in and out. Like people did during yoga. He'd seen it in movies.

"Okay. We're going to pretend you didn't say what you just said, and if you did, I didn't hear you. So, the way I see it, we have to somehow get out of here so you can contact the appropriate authorities, and the instant someone comes, we get you to a hospital."

Nick recoiled. He hated hospitals. "No!" He softened his voice because he'd yelled. "I don't need a hospital."

"You most certainly do. That gash is ugly, God knows how many microbes are in it, maybe Roman microbes, and it needs stitches. If you have a phobia for hospitals, I can call my doctor, who is good and has worked with psychiatric patients and understands phobias. He can stitch you up."

She turned before he could answer her.

Gah.

She'd turned the tables on him very neatly. It was the downside to being with a smart woman.

Nick wisely chose not to answer.

She'd walked to the back of the huge chamber. Nick estimated that there were at least a thousand rifles, including sniper rifles. Each cache was expected to support at least one resistance cell. There was a line of unbroken wooden boxes on brackets, no doubt also containing communications equipment, plastic explosives, ammo for the rifles and small arms.

Wait—he'd lost sight of Parker. He opened his mouth to call out to her when he heard her voice. "Nick!"

He hurried to the back of the chamber. There was another hatch, but the earth had moved more back here, and it was wrenched completely open. The hatch had detached from the hinges and lay on the dusty concrete floor. Beyond the hatch was a short passageway and the tunnel veered to the left and...yes! It was almost completely open to the sky.

Parker turned to him, blue eyes glowing. "Is this a direct enough connection?"

Nick already had his satphone up. Yes indeed, there was a connection.

He'd thought about this. He would eventually find the people at DOD, but Jacob Black had a direct line to the top brass. So Jacob was first call. Then Dylan, who would be transiting through Rome right about now.

Then the Consulate. As a courtesy, because this was not a consular affair, it was a military affair.

Jesus. Eight nukes. And thousands of arms.

The nukes alone would be a terrorist's wet dream. There were plenty of people in the Mediterranean who would kill to get their hands on eight nukes. Even old ones.

Because they were still workable. The military built nukes to last, though maybe not seventy years. The Davy Crocketts outside this cache had all been decommissioned. But the ones in this arms cache might still be viable in the hands of people who knew what they were doing. And modern terrorists all had enough money to hire the best people. And even if the nuclear weapons had degraded, there was quite enough uranium in them to create dirty bombs. New York, London, Paris—they could be rendered no man's land for generations.

These weapons had to be guarded with his life.

But not Parker's.

He had to find a way to get her out of here.

But first—Jacob.

Jacob Black. His partner and best friend besides Dylan. The three of them had fought together and bled together. Jacob would know who to call at the Pentagon. Nick avoided politics with fervor. Jacob hated politics too, but was better at the game. Jacob would cut through all bullshit and get the right people here as fast as was humanly possible.

Nick made the call. Jacob was the first on speed dial.

It shocked him a little to think that soon Parker would be first.

Jacob picked up immediately. "'Sup Nick?" he asked, his tone genial. His face was configured in weird lines, and it took Nick a second to realize that Jacob was *smiling*. Jacob Black defined serious and never smiled. Though, come to think of it, he smiled more and more since he'd gotten married to his wife, Alex Black.

"Broken Arrow," Nick replied, the phrase universally recognized as danger involving nuclear weapons. Jacob immediately looked serious and slightly pissed, his normal expression. He didn't ask Nick to repeat himself. He'd heard it well enough the first time.

Nick put the call on speakerphone.

"Sitrep!" Jacob barked.

"I'm in Naples. On Monday I start a contract to tighten security at the US Consulate. In the meantime, I'm helping the Consul's niece, who is working at the excavation of a Roman villa. Parker, meet Jacob Black. Jacob, meet Parker Donovan. She wrote and directed *The Smiling People*."

Jacob's eyes widened slightly, a sign of huge surprise for him. Nick knew Jacob loved the book and documentary. Nick angled his satphone so that Jacob could see Parker and Parker could see Jacob.

Jacob's expression didn't change when he saw Parker. He only had eyes for his wife.

"Mr. Black," Parker said.

"Jacob."

"Jacob, then. Nick kindly offered to help me as I was doing some research on a Roman villa that has just been discovered. We were caught in a bad earthquake about two hours ago. We've only now come to a position where we can call for help. But we also seem to have come across an arms cache. Nick tells me that eight of these weapons—which apparently date from the nineteen fifties—are nuclear weapons."

"Davy Crocketts," Nick said, "and some man portables." Jacob nodded.

"I'll leave the rest of the discussion to the two of you, but the thing you need to know, Jacob, is that Nick is badly wounded. He wouldn't tell you, but he is."

She grabbed the satphone and held it to Nick's left side, showing his bloody face and the open gash which had begun bleeding.

"It's nothing—" Nick began.

Parker shot him an angry glare and continued that glare when picking up the phone and scowling at Jacob. Not many people scowled at Jacob. "It's not nothing. Nick threw himself over me when he realized it was a major quake. We were at the bottom of the excavation of a room in the villa and a ton of rubble fell over Nick. He was bleeding copiously from his head wound and he has an open gash on his shoulder. I don't think he can pull himself up and I sure can't do it. So whoever comes will probably have to have some rope or something to pull him out. And I'm not leaving him, so that someone will have to be prepared to pull me out, too. And you need to send a medic."

"Understood, Dr. Donovan."

"Parker."

"Parker. I'm going to start mobilizing. Probably the first responders will be from elements of the Sixth Fleet stationed in Naples and they can take up guard duty and get you two out of there. And they will protect the site until the NEST people can arrive."

Parker nodded and handed the phone back to Nick. He should have been angry at her, but he found it hard. She was trying to protect him. It was crazy to think of someone protecting *him*, but she'd been right to let Jacob know that they'd probably need help getting out. He was too proud to say it, and it could get dicey trying to get them out.

"Show me the arms cache," Jacob ordered, and Nick walked slowly around, filming everything. Jacob would show it to his contacts in Washington.

Everything was old—at least seventy years old, but everything was in superb condition. The guns were well packed, and he could smell the gun oil. Everything neatly packed, ready to go. The supposition had been that resistance fighters and NATO soldiers would have immediate access to weaponry and comms to start fighting back the instant the Soviets attacked.

And there was enough here to start a small war. Even beyond the nuclear weapons. None of this could fall in terrorists' hands.

He finished the rounds and saw Jacob's grim face. Yeah. The weapons and explosives were old-fashioned, but they could do a hell of a lot of a damage.

"Okay," Jacob said. "I've seen enough. WhatsApp me that video. I'll get back to you as soon as I know something, ok? Stay safe. But then you have Parker to protect you."

He grinned suddenly and broke the connection before Nick could say anything. Nick ground his teeth.

Parker didn't notice. She had made the rounds of the space twice. "There's nothing really useful here, except for arms. And they aren't useful to us now. I wasn't expecting food or water but maybe a rope? A ladder? Our ladder is probably in a million pieces back in the Blue Room. What on earth are you doing?"

Nick looked up. He had an M1 Garand in his hand, which had been wrapped in oil cloth. In perfect condition. He lifted it one handed so he could peer down the sight. Then he picked up an FN FAL rifle, chambered in NATO rounds.

"Checking them. They are in prime condition. They work and cannot fall into the wrong hands."

She nodded her head. "Not to mention the nukes."

He put down the rifle. "Not to mention the nukes," he agreed.

Okay. He was going to try one last time. "Listen, I think if I stacked two boxes and got on top of them, I could boost you right out of here and—"

Parker rounded on him, blue eyes crackling fire. "Could you boost yourself?"

Could he boost himself? Nick measured distances with his eyes and felt his way through his body, which he knew inside out. "Maybe...not," he said. She just stared at him, arms crossed. "OK. Probably not."

"We're either both getting out or nothing. I thought I made myself clear. I've been told I express myself clearly. Few people have difficulty understanding what I say." Her jaw muscles moved, she was clenching her teeth in exasperation.

God. She was filthy, she'd crawled through dirt which clung to her face, hair and clothes. That crawl had ripped her blouse and pants. She looked like she'd been through a war.

And she was so beautiful it hurt to look at her. But that wasn't it. It wasn't just her beauty. She was proving to be the best possible partner—steadfast and helpful, even when she was mad at him. She'd come back for him when she could have just kept going. She didn't want to be rescued unless he could be rescued too.

He'd been fascinated by her and had had the best sex he could recall last night. But this was more. This felt like having a partner. This felt like what his parents had, an unbreakable bond. His mother could no more leave his father in a dangerous situation than she could fly.

Nick had been falling since he first laid eyes on Parker. Easy thing to do. She was fascinating, classy and gorgeous. But it was right now, with her glaring at him, covered with dirt, dinged and angry, that he slid all the way.

He gave in with a sigh, recognizing that his life was

going to be fundamentally different from here on. Everything had changed. And he also recognized that Parker very definitely had a will of her own and had no hesitation in speaking it.

He reached out and touched her shoulder. "Sorry. I wasn't listening to you. You told me over and over again you didn't want to leave me, and I let my emotions get the better of me. I hate the thought of you being here, in the rubble of an earthquake and in an Operation Gladio arms cache. A lot of things can go wrong, and I'm trained to think in terms of worst-case scenarios. But to tell you the truth, I'm really glad you're staying."

Her body language had changed. Her arms weren't folded tightly against her chest now, and she wasn't glaring at him. "You mean that?"

He nearly sighed. "With all my heart."

She rushed into his arms, jostling his wounded shoulder. Pain shot through him like a bolt of electricity. He gritted his teeth. It was a small price to pay to have her in his arms, not angry at him. They'd escaped death by a miracle. He'd been given a second chance.

"Oh," she mumbled into his torn shirt. "Now I can say how scared I was and still am. I couldn't say how scared I was and then run away like a rabbit."

Nick held her more tightly, head resting against hers. "Couldn't have that, no."

Parker sighed and relaxed into him, and they stood there, holding each other tightly. Parker was the first to step away. She sniffed, put a finger under her eyes where a little moisture had gathered—she'd absolutely reject the idea of that moisture being tears—and straightened.

"I think you're going to have to call Aunt Caroline."

"Yes." This was tricky. Because the Consul General didn't necessarily have the right to confidential military intel. There would be no protocol against it, but there wouldn't be a protocol for it.

But she'd be worried about Parker and that decided him.

He dialed her cell.

"Hello?" There was heavy background noise. She was either on the street or at the consulate with repair work going on. "Who is this?"

She wouldn't have the satphone's number in her cell's address book, only his regular work phone.

"Caroline," Nick said slowly. "This is Nick Garin. Please listen carefully. We have a Broken Arrow situation."

Silence.

Caroline would know exactly what that was.

"Where are you?"

"We're at Parker's excavation site. And during the quake we discovered an Operation Gladio arms cache underground."

She would know what Operation Gladio was and what could be contained in an arms cache.

"Are you both ok?"

"We're a little dinged, but essentially ok. I'm wounded and cannot pull myself out. I called Jacob Black to coordinate a military response."

She took a moment, and he gave it to her. There were a thousand unexpressed things here. Caroline would be a little miffed that he hadn't called her to organize a cordon around the arms. But she knew it wasn't really her call, and the Consulate was not officially involved. And the Consulate would definitely not have specialized personnel. The Consulate had some Marines but was mainly staffed by admins. She also knew Jacob Black would know exactly who to call.

"Right. Do you need anything?"

"Nothing that the Consulate can provide." The Consulate's Marine guards were good men, but there weren't enough of them. And the Marines could not desert the Consulate, particularly after a heavy earthquake.

"Right. So Parker's okay?"

"Yes."

"Make sure she stays that way," Caroline said and closed the connection.

"Is Aunt Caroline alright?" Parker asked, with a little frown of anxiety. "She hold up in the earthquake?"

"She seemed fine." Nick bent to kiss the frown away. "A little miffed I didn't call her first. And I have strict instructions to look after you."

"Call her first? Why would you call the Consulate first? Isn't this a military matter?"

She got it. "Exactly. I called her as a courtesy and probably shouldn't have. But I'm not in the military anymore and don't have a chain of command. I called Jacob Black because he knows exactly—"

Nick's satphone rang and he held up a finger, looking at who the caller was. Jacob, getting back to him. That was quick. Jacob had set it to a video call.

"Speaking of the devil... Hey what have you got?"

Jacob nodded. "The Naples Security Force from the Naples naval base is arriving right away to secure the site. They're en route. A NEST team from Norfolk is en route too, but they won't land until after midnight. NATO is scrambling its CBRN unit from Brussels. But you're free to go as soon as the Security Force gets there. They'll extract you and you get the hell out of Dodge. The Security Force will have a medic."

"Gladly get out of Dodge. And get Parker out of Dodge. Can't wait. But I don't know what state my vehicle is in."

"No problem. I'll let them know they need to provide a car and a driver. Someone will get your vehicle later. You guys okay?"

"Yeah. Will be good to get out of here, though."

Jacob gave a wintry smile. "Trust me. When the cavalry arrives, they won't want you there. They can't wait to get you out of there, either."

"Ditto."

"Oh, Dylan's coming, too. He was in Rome, wrapping up negotiations with Niram Shipping, as you know, and he's flying in, to help."

Dylan Gardner. Besides Jacob Black, his best friend. They'd fought together, bled together. But why the fuck—

"Wait." Nick scowled at the screen. "You told him I was wounded, didn't you?"

Jacob remained impassive. "Maybe."

"Damn." If Dylan thought Nick was in need and wounded, there was nothing in this life, or even after, that would keep him away. "So when is he arriving?" he asked, resigned. This excavation site was going to be busier than the train station in Rome, Stazione Termini.

Jacob checked his watch. "Probably in about an hour. I sent him your coordinates."

"Dylan loves skydiving. He'll probably jump out of the plane, land right on top of us."

"Probably. Keep me informed."

"You coming too?"

"Love to. But tonight Alex is getting some kind of science prize. Can't not be there. She'd dump my ass. I'll fly over tomorrow when it's all over."

His wife was as madly in love with him as he was with her. She definitely wouldn't dump his ass if he wasn't there when she got a prize. She was always getting prizes. But Jacob knew Nick was more than covered. If Nick were on his own, Jacob would already be on his way.

They'd always had each other's backs.

Which was why Nick loved his job, except the part where he had to deal with shithead psychopaths. That part sucked.

Jacob closed the connection.

"Nick?"

Parker. She must be exhausted. And thirsty. Nick was

thirsty too, and they had no access to water. He had several bottles in his SUV, but it could have been on the back side of the moon for all the good it did them.

But Parker wasn't complaining. She hadn't complained once. She was pale and dirty and dead on her feet, but with all that, focused on him. Her eyes kept going to the gash on his shoulder. It hurt, yeah, and needed disinfecting and stitching up, but he'd had worse.

"So," she said. "I guess now we wait for the cavalry to arrive."

B*roken Arrow!*

George Stillwell put his cell down. His hand was trembling. This was it. He knew exactly what Broken Arrow meant.

Nuclear weapons.

An Operation Gladio cache. He knew what that meant, too. Either a Davy Crockett or a man portable. Maybe both. Nineteen fifties stuff. Primitive, but nuclear.

This was it. That once in a lifetime opportunity. How to make best use of it? Pointless to offer it to the Russians. They were awash in nukes. They had so many they'd lost count of them. And sometimes they had even lost their location. The same for the Chinese. They had their own. But terrorists...that was something else. Even an old nuke, set off in the center of a city, would make a big statement. Could destroy a country if it was the right city. And if nothing else, the uranium could be used to create a dirty bomb.

And if he could get it into the right hands, he could ask for whatever he wanted. Shake the dust of these consulates from his feet and start living.

He knew who to call to start the ball rolling. A man who was clever and fast, because George knew soldiers from the Sixth Fleet would be arriving soon. They'd come and find crickets.

The man picked up before the first ring ended. Marco de Luca. "De Luca here."

The English was without an accent. He'd studied economics at Stanford and was the reason the Camorra was so rich. He was an expert in money laundering and knew how to invest.

He had perfect English and acceptable French. Wore Hugo Boss suits and Prada shoes and knew how to behave. He was also ruthless and cunning.

They said he was dating the niece of the President of the Italian Republic.

Smart and untouchable.

"Sir. We met at a party for an incoming consular officer."

Keep it vague. He knew his phone was unhackable, but though de Luca was smart and tech-savvy, you never knew. They'd met at a huge reception where Caroline Munro had been introduced to the top layers of Neapolitan society.

"Indeed. Cultural affairs attaché, I believe?"

That blew his cover. De Luca had done it deliberately. To show he knew George's identity and to compromise him. But George's end of the conversation wouldn't be recorded. When de Luca played it back, George's words would be static. Another really useful app.

Feeling time pressing, George got straight to the point. "There are eight nuclear weapons that have been uncovered by the earthquake. An Operation Gladio cache. At the moment they are unguarded, or rather guarded by one man and one woman, an historian, an expert on Rome. The man is a former soldier, but he is wounded. They have called it in to the Sixth Fleet and no doubt soldiers are on their way. If you get there first, you can grab eight nuclear weapons. They date back to the 1950s, but they would have been protected. And at any rate the uranium could be used for a dirty bomb. I don't have to tell you what one nuclear weapon is worth on the open market."

Silence.

A modern nuke would be worth upward of forty million dollars. Ten million at least for a 1950s weapon. Times eight. Its destructive power would be less, but a nuclear weapon set off in London or Paris or New York would be devastating. An attack for the history books. And nuclear material would go for at least two million dollars per kg.

"This is a time sensitive offer," George said cheerfully. He had the guy on a hook. "These opportunities come once in a lifetime. I can give you the coordinates where the nuclear weapons are, guarded only by two people. But as I said, the US military has been called in and they will be there soon. They will scramble, but it takes some time to put together a security team. If you leave right now, you will be in time to get there, eliminate the man and the woman, and grab the nukes. Sell them. There is a huge black market. What do you say?"

"How much do you want?" the voice asked cautiously.

"Ten million." He'd done his calculations. It was one eighth of the profit de Luca would make. If de Luca moved fast, eighty million dollars would drop in his lap with no effort beyond picking up the nukes and maybe eliminating two people.

Drugs, people trafficking, illegal toxic waste dumping —all of that was remunerative, but not as remunerative as this, and it was *work*. This wasn't work. This was sheer luck. Eight nukes dropping into his lap.

"How do I know you're telling the truth?"

"You don't. But I'm not stupid and I wouldn't lie to you about this. I wouldn't live to spend the money."

"True." There was a long pause. "Send me your bank details."

George entered his bank account number. "Done. An account number at a bank in Aruba. Once I get the money, I'll WhatsApp you the coordinates. Delete them as soon as you get them."

"Of course. Hold on while I send the money."

George waited until he heard a soft ping from his phone. He checked his account. He'd had close to a million dollars. Now he had just under eleven million dollars. That was fuck-you money.

"Got it," he said. "I'm sending you the coordinates." The coordinates had been in the phone call, Nikolai Garin sharing his location with Caroline Munro. Imagine her surprise and horror when Garin's body and the body of her niece were found at the bottom of the excavation of a Roman villa.

Oops.

With the added advantage that he could continue his monitoring of the Consul's phone for a while longer. Maybe get up to fifteen million before taking the app out.

Press for that posting to the Dubai Embassy. There would be endless opportunities for money making.

Life was good.

"Got the coordinates." De Luca's voice interrupted his reverie.

"Get there fast," George said and tapped the connection closed.

Nick took Parker's elbow and directed her to the concrete wall of the tunnel. "Let's sit down and wait for the cavalry."

She took one look at his face and nodded. Actually, Nick had been thinking of her, that she needed to rest. But the fact was he needed to rest, too. He didn't think he was concussed, but he had a raging headache and saw double if he moved his head too fast.

And of course, his shoulder hurt like a bitch.

So sitting sounded pretty good.

He grabbed a tarp that had covered a wooden case of M1 Carbines and shook it out. There was surprisingly little dust. The place had been sealed off for seventy years. He folded it several times so it would provide a cushion over the rough concrete and placed it on the ground. He stumbled slightly as he stood up. Damn! The world turned black for just a second.

But Parker noticed, and without making a fuss, helped him sit down on the floor and then sat down gracefully next to him.

It took him a moment to realize what the fuck had just happened. A woman had helped *him* down. Him. Nikolai Garin, aka Superman. Tough commando, temporarily as weak as a girl. It was humiliating.

He was holding Parker's hand with one hand and with the other was holding on to the ground.

Jesus, he *hated* feeling weak. Just hated it.

The blackness passed and his back straightened. He let go of the ground but not of Parker's hand.

She said nothing of the fact that she'd had to help him down like a child.

She looked over at him and gave a crooked smile. "Would be nice to have the cooler, wouldn't it?" And just like that, his appetite roared to life. Not just for food. The cooler with food was an hour's crawl away under a ton of rubble.

But Parker was right here.

With his free hand he turned her face to his and studied her. So dirty and dust-streaked and so very beautiful.

"What?" Parker asked.

"You're so beautiful," Nick sighed.

She laughed. "You really did get a blow to the head. A big one." Her expression changed. "I hope your friend Jacob Black didn't forget to ask for a medic for you."

"Honey, Jacob never forgets anything. Don't worry about that. And I'm not that bad."

She cocked her head. "You're a Monty Python sketch all by yourself. You know the one where the medieval knight gets his limbs lopped off and he hops up and down on his torso insisting he's fine?"

"Yeah." Nick rolled his eyes. He knew the sketch, and it was funny/sick. "Not that bad."

"Definitely that bad. You sustained a blow to the head, you probably have a massive headache—" she looked sternly at him until he reluctantly nodded his head, "—and you have a serious deep gash in your shoulder which needs cleaning out and stitching. And it's still *bleeding*. How is that not needing a medic?"

Nick stretched out his legs and put his arm around Parker. She sighed and leaned her head against his shoulder. The not-dinged shoulder.

"Would I win macho points if I said the shoulder is just a scratch?"

Parker huffed out a breath. "You most definitely would not. That's not just a scratch. You could have died.

I'm just glad you're alive. For a moment there, I was... scared."

Her voice wobbled for a moment, and Nick looked at her sharply. Her face was turned away and, though it hurt to move his left arm, he turned her face to him. Her eyes were wet. A tear escaped and moved down over that perfect skin.

She was crying. For him. Because she'd been worried about him.

Nobody worried about him, unless it was his teammates when he didn't respond to a check-in. Which had only happened once and because his radio had taken a bullet. Otherwise everyone assumed he could take care of himself. Which he could.

Nobody had to worry about him, except...having Parker worry felt sort of nice, though he'd shoot himself rather than say it. She cared. Of all the women he'd dated and bedded, he couldn't think of one who actually cared for him, as opposed to caring what he could do for them.

He was feeling a little shaky himself. They'd almost died. He'd realized in a flash that he was close to falling in love for the first time in his life. Was actually already there.

They'd stumbled across nukes.

It was a lot.

He needed to lighten things up. Nudged her with his shoulder. "Since we're waiting, can we fool around a little?"

Parker gasped then looked at his face, saw he was

joking. She hauled back a fist and swung it forward, stopping an inch from his chest.

"Glad you stopped," he said, relieved. "There isn't a place that doesn't hurt."

"Fooling around would have hurt."

"Worth it," he answered and she smiled.

"You know," she said as she put her head on his unwounded shoulder, "this is really scary, but sort of exciting, you know what I mean? If we make it out alive, it will be a really good story."

"Yup. You'll have to censor out the nukes, though, you know."

Parker sighed. "I imagined. The nukes give it extra special spice. But being buried during an earthquake in the remains of a Roman villa is still a great story. An exciting one. Maybe I missed my calling. Maybe I should have become a Navy SEAL."

"Maybe." Nick smiled at the thought. "But we get dirty a lot. Sometimes can't shower for weeks. Don't sleep in pretty flowered sheets and eat real crap. Sometimes have to go without sleep for days. Wear the same clothes for weeks. Sleep on rocks."

She shuddered. "I thought it was all adrenaline-inducing antics and dashing adventures. Parachuting out of planes and stuff."

He looked down at her. From this angle her face was super long eyelashes and sharp cheekbones. "Come to the dark side. We have cookies."

They laughed.

Oh man, he was so done. He bent and caught her mouth with his. A long, lush kiss, guaranteed to make him forget his aches and pains. Her mouth tasted delightful. Their tongues touched and it was like an electric wire pinged to life between his mouth and his groin.

He leaned lower, pressing against her, feeling excited and happy at the same time. Their situation was dire but not that dire. People were coming. If the earth could hold off on another quake for just another hour...

Nick's head lifted.

"What?" Parker murmured. Her eyes were still closed, mouth a little puffy from his.

"Someone's coming," Nick said, suddenly snapping back into reality.

"What?" Then Parker cocked her head. She heard it too. Engines, revving.

This was not good news. "Too early for the cavalry." He checked his satphone. "No messages. That's not the military from the Sixth Fleet."

Someone was coming for the nukes.

Nick stood up fast. One-handed, he stacked two crates right under the crack in the overhead ceiling. When Parker saw what he was doing she stood up and helped.

Nick moved quickly among the boxes and crates. There was a box that was regular gear, not arms, and he quickly found what he was looking for. He pulled out a pair of binoculars. Primitive by today's standards, just 7x50, but it had been state of the art in the 50s. Then he went to a crate and pulled out an M1 Garand, the old workhorse of NATO. It still had gun oil. He checked the action, and everything seemed to be in working order. There were ten boxes of 7.62 x 51 mm ammo. A thousand rounds. Enough to do damage. He picked out a Beretta BM 49 and placed it next to the M1 Garand.

Parker looked at him, eyes huge.

Nick positioned a big crate right under the opening then clambered up, very slowly and very painfully. He pointed to a smaller crate and Parker lifted it up to him. He climbed that one, too, even more painfully. His wound began bleeding again.

He could stick his head out of the opening. He didn't know if he could pull himself further up, whether his arm could take the strain. Probably not.

Nick put his hand down. "Can you hand me the binocs please?"

She held them up to him and he stuck his head up and glassed the area.

Oh fuck.

Three SUVs in a convoy, about a klick away, on the unpaved access road, a plume of dust following them. Those SUVs were exactly like his, like the ones the rental guy told him were used by the local mafia, the Camorra.

Mobsters had arrived for the nukes.

He texted Jacob. *Three SUVs coming, not military. Probably Camorra.*

Fuck. They either wanted the nukes for themselves or to sell to terrorists. Big big market.

Over his dead body.

. . .

Nick jumped down from the crates and it cost him. He didn't wince but she could tell he was hurting. Whatever he saw up there had galvanized him.

"What?" Parker asked. His face was impassive, but something was wrong.

"The people coming aren't the good guys. So until the cavalry arrives, we are the first line of defense."

The short hairs on her arms stood up. *They* were the first line of defense? A wounded man and *her?* She swallowed her dismay. She understood very well that they needed to defend those nuclear weapons, however primitive they were.

But still.

"Okay." Parker was proud to note that her voice was steady, though everything inside her quaked. "What do we do?"

Nick pointed to the back of the cavernous room. "You go hunker down behind the last cases. They are all gear of no use to anyone. Whoever's coming wants the nukes. If anything happens to me, stay hidden until our guys come. I'll text Jacob to tell them to look for you."

She was frightened to death, and angry, at the same time. "If the time comes when I have to hide, because something happens to you, God forbid, I'll hide. Or if there is a firefight. I don't know how to use a gun or fight. But until then, I'm helping you. I thought you understood that."

Nick winced. Though the face she'd seen on him so far was affable businessman and, last night, turned-on alpha male, this was different. She saw the soldier in him—brave and determined, even though he was wounded. Ready to die. She also saw, clearly, his fear for her.

He was right. She was scared, too, but she simply couldn't cower, not when she felt she could help him. If they were overpowered, she'd try to hide because she had no tools at all of self-defense. But she'd be worse off hunkering down somewhere while he defended them than trying to help. That was clear.

But he didn't want that. He wanted her safe. Which was a nice thought, but it wasn't a safe situation. Safe wasn't possible.

He was bent over his satphone, texting.

"The military is twenty minutes out, and Dylan has just landed at Capodichino Airport, he should be here in about half an hour. Maybe less."

"So, basically, we just have to resist for half an hour."

He just looked at her, grim-faced.

"I'm not minimizing the situation," she protested. "But —" she waved an arm around the huge warehouse. "Old or not, we're surrounded by weaponry. I can't shoot but I can, I don't know—hand you weapons? Do something to help you?"

His face suddenly melted. "Honey. Come here."

She walked into his arms and felt instantly safe. They *weren't* safe, not at all. Three SUVs were on the way. Technically that could mean twenty-one men, probably armed. Nick was one man. It was insane to feel safe just by holding him and having him hold her, but there it was. Humans were irrational, she knew that.

She hugged him more tightly, digging her face into his chest. Tears were very close to the surface. Before they could fall, she pulled away and made her voice sound matter of fact.

"Okay, tell me what to do."

He put a heavy hand on her shoulder. "When I tell you to hide, you hide. You have to promise me that."

She rolled her eyes. "Oh yeah, I promise. I'm not crazy. Where do I hide?"

"I told you. Against the far wall, past the flak jackets and gas masks. There's a big loose tarp. Hunker down and pull it over yourself."

She gave a sharp nod. "Gotcha. Past the flak jackets and gas masks. Tarp."

Usually her directions to friends were— *Two blocks down from Gucci and next door to Armani.* Past the gas masks and flak jackets was new.

He wasn't satisfied, a big scowl on his face. "Promise."

She crossed her heart. "Scout's honor."

"Were you a scout?"

"Not a chance. Were you?"

"Oh yeah. Made Eagle Scout."

She nodded, though she didn't have the faintest idea what that meant.

Nick gave a sharp nod then exploded into action. Ten rifles were lined up in a neat row, bullets having been fed into an internal part of the rifle. His movements were so fast she could hardly keep up. Then he lined up ten pistols fully loaded. He'd said they were Berettas, which she knew was an Italian firm. They looked pretty stylish.

"Here." To her surprise, he held one out to her, butt first. Parker resisted the childish impulse to put her hands behind her back. She'd never touched a gun in her life.

She took it gingerly.

"Careful," he said. "It's loaded."

Parker nearly jumped but contained herself. This was a new world, but she was living in it and had to adapt. Rome fell because it couldn't adapt. She had no intention of falling.

Nick picked up a gun identical to the one she was holding. "Hold it like this."

He showed her his hold, though his hand was so big it almost completely covered the important bits. Nonetheless, the gun was designed for human hands, and she had one of those.

She picked it up and it somehow...fit.

"Excellent," Nick said. "Now take the safety off."

He pointed out a little lever up top which she thumbed up and a little red dot appeared. "Red for dead," he said. "Now it's ready to shoot."

He held his gun up to eye level, aiming at the wall. He had a two-handed grip, left over right. "There's a sight at the end of the barrel. Put what you're shooting at in the sight."

Parker nodded *yes*, lifting her gun, trying to emulate his two-handed grip.

He moved her gun to the left with a finger, away from him.

"Make sure you don't shoot *me*."

"No, no!" She shook her head frantically.

"I'm going to go back up, see what position they are in."

Nick found a small tarp and held it in his hand.

Parker moved fast to put the big crate right under the big crack in the ceiling. Nick climbed up. He moved more slowly, and his arm was covered in blood. You could not tell anything from his expression, but he must have been hurting badly.

Parker held the smaller crate up as high as she could and he took it from her, together with the binoculars.

He climbed up the smaller crate, carefully placed the tarp over his head and slowly, slowly, poked his head up.

Parker nearly danced in place with anxiety. She had trouble breathing, her heart felt like it would beat its way right out of her chest. Where were those people? Who were they if they weren't the cavalry? If they were organized crime—

"Aunt Caroline really must have a security issue. I think someone must have listened in on her call."

"Yup," he said quietly. "And I think the people out there are gangsters. They are all armed. One is consulting a GPS reader. But I don't think he knows how it works. That will buy us some time."

"Oh God." Parker covered her face with her hands.

"This is all my fault. You called Aunt Caroline to reassure her that we were safe after a major earthquake, to make me feel better. If you hadn't called her, we'd just be waiting for the soldiers, not waiting to fight off mobsters or terrorists. I'm so sorry."

He didn't look down at her, binoculars glued to his face under the tarp. "Actually, I probably did have to call the Consulate, since technically I'm under contract to them. If nothing else, this is proof that the Consulate has a security issue. Which is nice to know, even if it costs us our heads being blown off."

Parker peered up at him. "Are you saying that just to make me feel better, less guilty, or is it true?"

Nick removed the binoculars and looked down at her. Crazily, he grinned. They were in a terribly perilous situation, but he was trying to reassure her. "I would say it just to make you feel better, but it's also true." He brought the binoculars to his eyes again. This time his voice was cold, emotionless. "Parker, hand me one of the rifles."

She picked it up by the barrel and was about to lift it to him when he closed his eyes in pain. "Can you hand it to me by the stock?"

"The stock? What—"

And then of course she got it. She was about to hand him the rifle in a way where she could blow his face off if she handled it wrong. She held it up to him, stock-first, and he took it, stowing it on top of another crate. At no point in his handling of the rifle had the barrel been pointing at her.

She'd probably have blown his face off.

She was tired, scared, completely out of her depth. But she needed to up her game if she was going to be useful.

"What's happening?" she whispered.

"They are still trying to figure out the coordinates. I see twelve men, all armed." His voice was low, not a whisper.

She tried to suppress a shudder. Twelve men. Armed. They were so in trouble if the military didn't arrive soon. No way could Nick, alone, keep twelve armed men at bay. He'd go down fighting, but he'd go down.

Something buzzed in his pants, and he took out his satphone and reported on the messages. "The military will be here in ten minutes. Dylan is choppering in."

Parker covered her mouth with her hand. "Won't they shoot at a helicopter?"

"Don't worry." A corner of Nick's mouth lifted. "He'll be shooting back."

"So—if we can remain undetected, we might make it?"

"We'll make it in any case," Nick said, no stress in his voice at all. He believed it. Oh man, she wanted to believe it too. The cavalry plus Nick's friend were coming. And she had Nick right here.

Nick was like a little army, all by himself.

She was so impressed. He moved painfully but with purpose, knowing exactly what should be done and how to do it.

But they were in a hole in the ground, two against twelve. Like the Greeks against the Persians at Thermopylae. *They* all died. She and Nick might die, too. She had no desire to die today, none. Not after having met the most fascinating man in the world, not when, throughout the danger, she could feel the *Apocalypse Then* book coming together. A new man and a new book. She wanted to live for both.

He covered his head again and slowly peered over the edge. So carefully that Parker was sure that unless you were looking directly at him you couldn't see him.

"What's happening?"

He didn't whisper like she did, just spoke in a low voice. "Still searching for the coordinates. They'll get here eventually." He checked his watch. "Five minutes. All we have to do is survive another five minutes. Easy peasy."

He stood stock still for a minute, two. "Damn," he said. "They figured it out. They are walking our way. Go to the back wall and pull that tarp over yourself." Parker started walking to the back wall. "Don't forget to keep the Beretta with you."

Oh God. The gun. Yes, she needed to keep the gun on her, though just imagining a situation where she'd need to shoot the gun—shoot a person— terrified her. She grabbed one of the pistols—a Beretta, though she wouldn't have been able to tell the difference between a Beretta and any other gun before today.

Because much as she didn't want to use it, she would if she had to.

Nick jumped down from the top crate though it must have jarred his shoulder terribly. He glanced up at the opening and took the time to cover the array of weaponry he'd amassed—rifles, pistols, hand grenades—with a tarp.

Making it look like it was carelessly flung there, not like it was covering things. He went to the opposite corner from her.

She understood that if necessary to keep her safe, he'd give up his position to draw attention away from her.

He turned off the flashlight app. It was completely dark inside the chamber, the only light coming from the broken ceiling. She was crouching against the wall, the tarp covering her loosely. She'd created what looked like a fold but was actually a break that allowed her a partial view.

She could hear male voices, excited, speaking in Neapolitan dialect.

Her heart beat so hard she was surprised they couldn't hear it up top. It beat against her rib cage in hard thumps. There were twelve armed men up top, who wanted something in the cavern very badly. They were criminals who wouldn't hesitate to kill them for what they wanted.

Nuclear weapons. Oh God. Nuclear weapons in the hands of criminals, maybe terrorists. The damage they could do was unthinkable.

It wasn't beyond the realm of imagination that they could bring down civilization. A few nuclear weapons set off in major cities and the world would be lost. Rome was brought down by barbarians wearing bear skins and wielding hatchets. The most powerful military in history brought low. By primitives who were unrelenting.

Those nuclear weapons could cause their world to collapse. No more electricity, no more medicine, no more education. No more printing presses or theater or art. Just brutality and ignorance for generations.

She was a scholar of the fall of Rome. It had happened once, and it could happen again.

She and Nick were all that stood in the way of that until the US military and Nick's friend could arrive.

The thought of another Dark Ages, lasting maybe a thousand years—it simply could not be.

She realized, to her surprise, that she was willing to die to prevent that.

A man stuck his head down, followed by his arm. He was holding a flashlight. He carefully shone it around the room, but missed her and missed Nick, wherever he was hiding.

He shouted to the men behind him—*they're here. The weapons*.

The enemy had arrived.

Eleven

Unless Nick did something, the mobsters were still in time to steal the nukes and disappear. They might have a solid chance. There would be a massive manhunt, but they knew the terrain and would have safe houses. There was an outside chance that they could get away with it.

That would not happen. Nick had an arsenal at his disposal, including grenades. But he also had Parker to protect. He'd never gone into battle with any thought other than winning. Winning was essential but so was protecting Parker. It felt like he was at war with himself, because many of the tactics he could use could endanger her.

He had to take it second by second.

They're here! He texted Jacob, knowing he would convey it immediately to the troops coming. They hadn't even had time to set up separate direct comms, the only way to reach the military was through Jacob.

The answer came back almost immediately. *Almost there.*

Okay. All he had to do was survive and make sure Parker survived too. If he had to, he'd direct attention to himself across the chamber, signal to Jacob that Parker was here.

There was noise up top, the gangsters conferring. He wished Parker were here so she could interpret for him, but they were just figuring out how to get in and get the nukes out. Not easy. The crack in the casing was barely big enough for a person to get through. The Davy Crocketts were wide, heavy, unwieldy. So were the man portables. The military would be coming with equipment, but the mobsters had clearly been told to get here fast and would only have shooting weapons. They could aim their machine guns all they wanted at the concrete. They weren't getting the nukes out easily, and when the military arrived, they weren't getting the nukes out at all.

But shit happens, nobody knew that better than Nick. And whatever happened, those weapons would never fall into hands other than the US military. Just wasn't going to happen.

A young man stuck his head into the opening. Dark-haired, handsome, lithe. Somehow, he wriggled his way down, feet first, hands holding on to the concrete. It was a long way to fall, and he was studying how to do it when Nick took him out.

Two shots, center mass. The young man fell in a boneless heap to the ground twelve feet below.

Nick could hear the murmur of voices, a little shocked. This wasn't going to be as easy as they thought, and they knew there was a timeline. And that someone armed was down with the weapons.

Damn right, Nick thought. He had an almost endless arsenal and hand grenades. He would be sitting pretty if it weren't for Parker, across the cavernous area, vulnerable.

He was sitting behind a big metal chest, in shadow, against the curved concrete wall. Invisible, unless they had night vision. The man who'd volunteered to go first hadn't had night vision, just a Beretta AR 70/90 on a sling.

And then, to his horror, an assault rifle appeared, the hand holding it above the line of concrete, so he couldn't shoot the hand. The hand was holding another Beretta AR, only it had a drum. A drum that could hold 100 bullets.

His blood froze. He was behind a steel container. Parker was behind a tarp. Nick was up and running before he could think and had flung himself over Parker when the gangster started shooting. He sprayed the area continuously, the sound of bullets pinging loud in the enclosed space.

Nick spread himself, covering as much of Parker as he could, hands over her head.

Something punched him hard in the back. The sound of gunfire stopped, casings still clinking to the ground.

Nick lifted himself up, arms trembling. It was harder than expected. For some reason, he couldn't hold himself up.

"You okay?" he asked, his voice weak.

Parker turned a terrified face to him. She looked at the ground, which was turning red, then at him. "I'm okay but you've been shot!"

He'd been shot? What the fuck?

And then all the pain in the world rushed in to sandbag him. It had been masked by adrenaline but now he felt it.

He clenched his teeth against the groan.

Parker's eyes widened and he looked up. One of the mobsters, slim, lithe and athletic, dangled by one hand then dropped to the dirt, standing up immediately. He walked around, and Nick saw the exact moment he was spotted. The man was young, elegantly dressed, with a good haircut. Handsome, with empty eyes.

The mobster started walking toward them, bringing up the assault rifle to his shoulder. There wasn't anything Nick could do. He'd dropped his weapon to be able to get to Parker faster and he was glad he did. The bullet that had gotten him would have gotten Parker. But now he couldn't defend her. He was weak, bleeding, weaponless.

The man seemed to be almost enjoying himself as he sauntered toward them. It would be like shooting ducks in a barrel. Nick was wounded and he was unarmed. Clearly Chic Mobster hadn't seen Parker and Nick was desperate to keep it that way.

Outside was a commotion. The sound of a helicopter, men shouting orders, a gunshot or two. It didn't seem to faze Chic Mobster. Maybe he thought it was his people, but Nick knew what it was. Dylan's chopper and the arrival of US troops. Here to guard the weapons until NEST came.

It was over. The nukes were safe. The good guys had won. *He* wouldn't win, though. Nobody could make it inside before the gangster shot him more full of holes than he was already. But with some luck, Parker might make it out alive.

As he continued sauntering toward them, Nick said, very low, "He hasn't seen you. Don't move. Stay under me after he finishes shooting."

Hoping the bullets didn't go through him and hit her.

Oh God.

Fuckhead slowly brought the gun up to his shoulder, clearly enjoying himself. Shooting an already wounded, unarmed man was fuckhead heaven. Nick was dying anyway. He was losing a lot of blood, and his head was feeling woozy. The edges of his vision were turning black.

Nick braced, because bracing against a bullet traveling two thousand feet per second did so much good. Fuckhead got a good grip on his rifle and put his trigger finger on the trigger, smiling widely.

Shitheads lived for moments like these. Where they could inflict pain and suffering with no consequences.

The noise level outside was increasing, shouts and loud engine noises, but fuckhead wasn't even noticing. He aimed down the barrel and Nick said his goodbyes to life and...

The fucker's head exploded while big chunks were blown out of his chest.

He fell where he stood, deader than dirt.

Parker still had a death grip on her gun. Pistol. Whatever it was called. She had to consciously relax her fingers, one by one.

She'd just shot a man. Twice. Something she'd have said was impossible, but there he was, bleeding in the dust, unmoving. And the most astonishing thing of all was that she wasn't sorry. Not one bit.

Until the day she died, she'd never forget the expression on his face, evil and gloating. About to shoot the finest man she'd ever known.

She was hidden beneath Nick, who'd run faster than she'd ever seen anyone move to throw himself over her, to shield her, but she had a narrow view encompassing the gangster slowly walking toward Nick, clearly enjoying every second of planning the death of someone defenseless. Already wounded and unarmed. The guy didn't know she was there, and Nick was prepared to sacrifice his life to make sure the man didn't know she was there.

She was hidden. But...she had a gun. Nick was *not* going to be killed by a cruel baby gangster in an Armani suit and with a trendy haircut. Not if she could help it.

He was so close, she couldn't miss. She was hidden in shadows and partially shielded by the tarp. He lifted the rifle to his shoulders, readying himself to kill Nick.

Over her dead body.

Fast, because if she didn't move fast, they were lost, she lifted the pistol, which was black and wasn't reflecting light. She could tell the gunman didn't see it. He was fully focused on Nick.

She flipped the safety—*red is dead*—lined the sights up with his chest, just like Nick had taught her, and pulled the trigger twice. And cheered to herself when she saw two big holes open up in his chest.

And then—his head exploded! She hadn't done that. What—?

"Parker!" a voice shouted. An American voice, deep and commanding like Nick's. "Parker Donovan! I'm Dylan Gardner, Nick's friend. Don't shoot me."

She hadn't even noticed someone peeking out from the big crack, carrying a gun.

Nick's friend! With a sob she crawled out from under Nick, as a tall, broad-shouldered man lowered himself from the ceiling with one hand, holding an assault rifle in the other. He dropped lightly to the floor. Parker ran to him, crying, and grabbed his arm.

"He's hurt! Oh God, Nick's been shot!"

He held her by the shoulders, looking her up and down. She was covered in blood. "Are you hurt? Have you been shot too?"

"No!" She gave a huge sob. "It's Nick's blood. We have to get him to a hospital immediately!"

Dylan rushed past her to Nick, hunkered down beside him. He ripped Nick's shirt and carefully examined the wound in his back, then lifted him so he could see Nick's chest.

His face was drawn and sober. He looked over his shoulder at her and she could read his expression as if he said the words aloud. *It's bad.*

"Didn't punch through," he said, lifting away a backpack she hadn't noticed. And bless him, the backpack had medical supplies. He pulled out things she didn't recognize and placed them on the tarp. "Hey big guy." He slapped Nick's face lightly. "Open up those big baby blues. This is going to hurt."

Nick looked barely conscious, but he nodded. "Dylan," he murmured.

"That's right." Dylan pulled out what looked like pads and pressed two over the bullet wound on the back. And pressed down hard. Nick closed his eyes and bit his teeth. The pads filled with blood immediately and Dylan pressed two more. It took six pads before the bleeding stopped. Dylan took a long strip of gauze and wrapped it tightly around Nick's abdomen. He then tapped his ear and said, "Come down."

There was a crack, a big chunk of the concrete fell to the floor and two men rappelled down. They were carrying something that unfolded into a litter, saw Dylan, and hustled over. One looked over at her, covered in dust and blood.

"Ma'am?"

She waved her hand at Nick. "I'm not wounded, he is. See to him."

They both turned back to Nick. They were tying Nick to the litter with complicated knots. Parker hovered, crying, holding on to Nick's hand. His eyes were half open but unfocussed. She was terrified he was slipping away.

"Ma'am?" the same man said.

Parker didn't understand.

The man pointed to their joined hands. "We need to move him now."

She was clinging to his hand, and they couldn't move him. How could they get him up? She reluctantly let his hand go, hating it. She wanted to be connected to him. He wouldn't die if she was holding his hand.

All of a sudden there was a loud thunk and another big piece of the concrete ceiling broke away. The opening was large. Several men rappelled down fast on ropes. Two stood at attention holding ropes. When the two soldiers carrying Nick brought his litter to where men were pouring in, the two men holding ropes efficiently tied them to Nick's litter, at the head and the feet. One whirled his index finger and Nick's litter rose, smoothly, to the top.

Hands grabbed the litter at the top and he disappeared.

Parker panicked. "I want to go with Nick!" she said, her throat tight.

Dylan was at her side. "Here, step into this." He was holding ropes tied in knots into a strange shape. He held it for her and indicated she was to step into it. At the end, she was fitted into a sort of harness. He clapped his hands, looked up and nodded.

She was hauled up quickly and smoothly and swung

out onto the ground. A female soldier helped her out of the harness. "So how are—" she began but Parker took off running. They were carrying the litter to the helicopter, and she was going to be on that helicopter or die.

Soldiers were swarming everywhere, moving purposefully. She had no idea what they were doing, and she didn't care. The nukes were safe. Now all she cared about was Nick. White-faced, eyes closed, hand dangling over the side of the litter.

He was being loaded onto the helicopter. She put her foot on the step and one of the soldiers in the helicopter put up his hand. "Sorry, ma'am."

Parker knew she must look like a madwoman—filthy and bloodstained and with a wild look in her eyes. But she was willing to go berserk. She was not leaving Nick's side.

The man who'd stopped her looked past her, nodded, and held out his hand. She took it and was hauled up and into the helicopter. Right behind her was Dylan. There were six seats facing each other and Nick was lying on his litter in the middle. Parker was horrified to see that he was starting to bleed through the bandages Dylan had applied. There were two soldiers, and one started removing the bandages. When he'd removed them, he sterilized the area around the wound then placed new bandages.

Parker had no idea how to help so she sat and held Nick's hand. He was unconscious and wouldn't notice, but it made her feel better.

They had taken off as soon as everyone was on board,

and they were traveling low and very fast. Conversation was impossible over the noise.

Dylan handed Parker a crash helmet. When she put it on, he indicated a button on the side. When she pressed it, his voice came on as if he were sitting right next to her and talking in her ear.

"We're heading to the US Naval Hospital in Naples, Parker. A surgical team is standing by. Nick will be taken directly into the operating theater. He'll be ok. He's tough."

Parker lifted her eyes to his, miserable. "He's lost so much blood," she whispered. To her surprise, he heard. The internal comms system was very good.

"That's why he's being transfused right now. His blood type is on file."

She looked at the second man, who was unpacking a box with IV bags of blood. He had an IV tree, hung the bag, and slid a needle in the crook of Nick's arm. Nick's eyes didn't even move beneath his lids.

Oh God.

The medic opened up the tube and blood started traveling into Nick's arm. Undoubtedly saving his life.

She gripped Nick's hand more tightly. If she could, she'd infuse him with her own life force. But she couldn't. She couldn't do anything but hold his hand and hope that somewhere deep inside him, he knew she was with him.

Because she loved him.

There was no denying that fact. When she'd dreamed

of finding love, she thought it would take time. Days, weeks, months. Maybe even years. She was picky, had only a few friends, had moved around the world and didn't have a crew of friends. So she didn't know how good a handle she had on people. Usually, she preferred books.

But nothing in her life prepared her for the heart-wrenching feelings she had for Nick. In the short span of time they'd known each other, he'd proved to be kind, gentlemanly, a sex god in bed, and willing to die for her.

Smart and honorable.

She loved him and recognized the feeling because she'd never felt anything remotely like this before. It was a mixture of warmth and fierceness. She'd killed the man who wanted to shoot Nick—well, Dylan had killed him as well—and she was glad. She'd do it again. And again. To defend Nick.

"We're approaching Naval Hospital in Naples," she heard Dylan say in her helmet. "There's a surgical team waiting for him. He's going to get the best possible care. He's a bit of a legend in the military. Not only was he an outstanding soldier, but he's saved eight nukes from the hands of terrorists. You, too."

She waved a hand. She hadn't done anything, really.

"He'll definitely get a medal. Another one. I wouldn't be surprised if you got one, too."

Parker shook her head. She didn't want a medal. She wanted Nick, alive.

She felt Dylan's touch on her arm.

"There's one thing that has to be made clear, though, Parker. Look at me."

His voice turned very deep and serious. Startled, Parker raised her eyes from Nick's face to look at Dylan. His features were as serious as his voice.

"Listen to me very carefully, Parker. If you and Nick get medals, they are the kind that can never be shown to anyone and have to be locked away. Nick's got a lot of those. You're a public figure, but you can never talk about this. I was told that the mobsters who were sent out belonged to the de Luca clan and they are vicious and vengeful. If it got out that you two were responsible for saving the nukes, and thwarting the de Lucas, your life wouldn't be worth living. They'd put out contracts, and when you least expect it, killers would come for you. So, I'll need your word of honor that you will never discuss this publicly, ever."

Parker shuddered. The idea of having mobsters after them... "You have it. Oh my God, yes. I wouldn't want to relive this, anyway."

"Swear to it."

"Oh yes." She held up her hand. "I swear I will never speak a word of this to anyone."

"There would also be legal consequences. For betraying state secrets. You can't be court martialed, but you could be tried for treason."

Still with one hand up, she mimed zipping her mouth with the other. Completely serious. If Nick survived, she'd never speak of it again. If he didn't survive, she'd be so devastated she'd spend years in mourning. Never wanting to relive what had cost him his life.

"Okay," Dylan said, and she turned back to Nick, on his back, wounded, being transfused.

She took his hand again and his eyes fluttered. Yes! She bent, put her cheek next to his.

"Live, my darling," she whispered. "Live."

Twelve

They made it to the Naval Hospital as the sun was setting. Lights were switching on around the helipad as they landed. The pilot brought them in gently, and Parker could see paramedics waiting with a proper gurney, ducking from the backwash. They moved in the instant the pilot switched off the rotors.

In a minute, Nick was gently removed from the floor of the helicopter, placed on the gurney together with the IV tree and bag of blood, and they took off at a run. Parker wanted to follow, but Dylan kept her back with a hand.

"Just a minute, Parker. You won't be able to follow him into the operating theater. There will be a waiting room, we'll go there. He's in good hands."

What he said made sense, but Parker had the horrible feeling her presence was keeping Nick alive and if they were separated, Nick would pay horrible consequences. But that was her panic talking.

A female officer appeared, tall, slender, dark brown hair in a tight bun, walking quickly toward them. "Dr. Donovan? Mr. Gardner? This way please."

Parker walked down the steps onto the tarmac and almost fell. Her legs could barely keep her upright. Dylan reached out a steadying hand until she was stable. "Sorry," she said.

He shook his head sharply. "You've been through hell, Parker. I'm surprised you're still standing." He looked her up and down. She was filthy with blood-encrusted clothes. "You look like you've been through a war."

Yeah. Buried by an earthquake, crawling through rubble, finding an arms cache with nuclear weapons, a shootout. She'd also shot and killed a man. Maybe. Maybe she'd shared that experience with Dylan. "I have."

"If you'll follow me," the female officer said. They followed her into the hospital facility, down a corridor and up two floors. She stopped at a door and ushered them into a small but welcoming room with upholstered armchairs. "I'll have beverages and some sandwiches sent up."

Parker's stomach revolted at the idea of food.

"Where's Mr. Garin?" she asked the officer.

"My understanding is that he is being prepped for surgery. The surgeon is Dr. Bernard Crowley, who is an excellent surgeon. He's in very good hands, ma'am."

Parker nodded. She'd acknowledge that Nick was in very good hands when he was out of surgery, and she could see that he was alive and well with her own eyes. Until then she was going to seethe in anxiety.

They took their seats. Parker sank into herself, inside her a maelstrom of terror and exhaustion. Dylan didn't even try to talk to her. He must have sensed that she didn't want to talk. All she wanted was for the surgeon to come down and say Nick was out of surgery and was going to be fine.

Anything else was unthinkable.

The female officer returned with a cart filled with sandwiches, soft drinks, tea and coffee.

"You should eat something, Parker," Dylan said gently.

"No thanks." She shook her head sharply, her stomach heaving. "I'll have some tea." Her own antibiotic. Tea cured so many things.

Dylan poured her a cup. "Sugar? Milk?"

She shook her head no.

Dylan was stacking a small plate with sandwiches and poured himself a Coke. "We're getting the super white glove treatment. They don't usually offer refreshments in the waiting room. It's because we're heroes. Nobody knows quite why, but they know we're heroes."

Parker didn't feel like a hero. She felt like someone who had escaped something terrible, and Nick had paid the price for it.

Nick had to live.

She kept coming back to that idea. Nick simply couldn't die. She wouldn't let him.

Dylan kept getting phone calls, and he'd exit the room so he wouldn't bother her. Either that, or the calls were confidential. She didn't care either way.

He came in, staring at his phone. "So, Nick was hired to check if there were any leaks in the Consulate and he got the job done. In a roundabout way."

Parker looked at him. What was he talking about?

"We had our in-house computer genius analyze the Consul's phone and it was hacked. There was a hidden app that sends all the calls and texts the Consul receives to a specific phone. And we were able to locate that phone and it did indeed belong to a consulate staffer. George Stillwell. Who immediately called Lorenzo de Luca, the local head of the Camorra. That Stillwell guy is going away forever."

Parker stared. "George? George Stillwell? A traitor?"

"Yes, ma'am. And he's been selling secrets for a while now and has a nice little stash in Aruba which he will never spend."

She sat with that for a while. George Stillwell. Weedy, ineffectual George. George, who couldn't play sports, could barely drive, but who was super smart. But how smart was he really if he was going to spend the rest of his life in prison?

"I can hardly believe he'd have the nerve."

"Well, he did. And if not for you and Nick, we could have eight nukes in the hands of either the mob or, more likely, they'd have sold them to terrorists. Lots of groups in the Mediterranean with money who'd pay a lot to have nuclear weapons. You guys stopped something really serious."

Parker didn't know what to say.

Dylan touched her arm. "Though you do understand that you can't ever talk about it, ever. To anyone. That's clear to you, right?"

"Absolutely." As long as Nick lived through his ordeal, Parker didn't even want to remember it. As long as—

The door opened and a short, stubby man with a salt and pepper beard walked in, carrying something. He was in scrubs, a surgical mask around his neck. "Dr. Donovan? Mr. Gardner?"

They turned to him. "Dr. Crowley?" Dylan asked.

"Yep." He didn't turn to Dylan but to Parker. "Dr. Donovan, I couldn't believe my ears when someone said that Parker Donovan was in the waiting room. It is such an honor to meet you. My wife and I loved *The Smiling People*. We've read the book and watched the documentary. My congratulations."

He held out his hand and Parker just looked at it. Then took it and he pumped her hand up and down enthusiastically.

"Beautifully written and beautifully filmed. We enjoyed it tremendously." He held out his other hand and she recognized what he was holding. A book. *Her* book. "We would both be honored if you could sign the book."

Dylan looked amused. "And we'd both really like news about our friend, Nikolai Garin."

The doctor was holding the book out, open to the title page. "If you could just sign here..." He pushed his glasses up to the bridge of his nose. "As for Mr. Garin," he said casually, "he'll be fine. The bullet missed all vital organs.

In fact, the biggest danger was blood loss, but he was transfused during the medevac flight, which mitigated the blood loss."

Parker felt numb. "He'll—he'll live?"

"Oh, yes." The doctor blinked. "Yes indeed. He'll be out of the hospital in a day or two. Now if you could just sign here..." He held out a pen. "To Bernie and Esther."

Parker's knees felt weak and again she felt Dylan's steadying hand. Tears sprang into her eyes as she signed and a big fat drop plopped onto the page, right where she'd written Parker.

"Oh! I'm so sorry! I can get you another copy!"

Dr. Crowley just shook his head. "That's fine. Don't worry about it. I understand you're worried about your friend, Mr. Garin." He touched her forearm and smiled and looked her up and down. "He'll be ok. You know, it will be a couple of hours before you can see him. You might want to change out of those bloody clothes. I understand it is his blood, so maybe he won't want to be reminded of being shot."

Parker looked down at herself. She'd completely forgotten what she looked like. Filthy from crawling through rubble, and caked with Nick's blood. Now that she knew Nick was going to live, her skin itched with the desire to shower and change.

"A car and a driver are waiting outside for you," Dylan said. "If you could pick up Nick's things from the hotel, that would be great. I called the hotel to have them packed for him. I'll wait here for you."

Parker turned to the doctor. "I want to be here when Nick wakes up and can receive visitors."

"You will be," the doctor said gently. "Unless you live in Rome."

"I live on the Vomero."

"Then you'll make it. Go on then. You'll feel better afterwards, and Mr. Garin will feel better not seeing his blood on you."

Well...put that way...

"I'll be here," Dylan said, "And he will be out of it for another—"

He looked at Dr. Crowley. "I'm not allowing anyone in for at least another three hours. Mr. Garin is currently in the recovery room and will be for a while. Then he will be taken to his hospital room, but I like to give patients time before they are allowed visitors. And he'll be a little loopy from the anesthesia for a while anyway."

Dylan put his hand on her shoulder. "The driver is in the parking lot and has your name on a tablet he'll hold up. He will wait for you at the hotel and then he will wait for you at your house and will drive you right back here. Go."

She went.

Like everything connected to Nick, it all went super smoothly. The driver, a very nice Italian gentleman, was in the parking lot, offered her a bottle of water she hadn't realized she wanted until he handed it to her, and took off. He navigated Neapolitan traffic like a pro. Which she supposed he was. When they got to Nick's hotel, the driver insisted she stay in the car while he got Nick's suitcase and came back in a quarter of an hour, pushing a big hardcase wheelie.

He miraculously found a parking spot right outside her gate and told her to take however long she wanted. He'd wait for her.

Parker's hands were shaking but she didn't want to let the nice Italian gentleman know that. She murmured something, dropped the key to the street door, picked it up, got into the building, ran up the steps, fumbled the key to her apartment door, finally got it open and slammed it behind her.

She shed her filthy clothes as she ran to the bathroom, stepping out of her panties just as she entered the shower stall, and turned the water as hot as she could get it and stood under the stream, crying, until she got it out of her system.

She had no idea why she was crying. She and Nick had both survived something terrible, but they were okay. But as long as she lived, she could never forget that moment when Nick came flying at her, covering her with his body, and the feel of the punch as the bullet hit him.

For one horrible moment, she thought she'd lost him, as the blood poured out of him. That she hadn't lost him was a miracle, but she understood that as he raced toward her, throwing himself over her, he was consciously sacrificing himself. Shielding her with his body, fully prepared to die. For her.

It didn't bear thinking about. She sat on the floor under the shower head, legs pulled up against her chest and sobbed. The tears came in great wracking gulps of air, almost spasms. She cried and cried until she couldn't breathe, until no more tears came, until her chest hurt.

She sat against the shower wall until her sobs ceased, and her breathing returned to normal. She sat for a long time, thinking of nothing, mind completely empty. Letting the hot water pour over her, warming her up from the bones out.

Though it was a hot day, she'd been freezing. Shock, no doubt. But now she was warm again.

Parker stood up, easily. Her legs had been unsteady when she walked into her apartment, but now they carried her easily. She felt light, as if the crying jag had liberated her from a black bolus of evil. She turned the water off and stood there, herself again. Suddenly, she couldn't wait to get back to Nick. It felt like her life had split into two. Before Nick and now with Nick, and she needed to be by his side, right now.

They'd both survived something that should have killed them. The earthquake and the shootout, either one. But they weren't dead. They were alive, and Parker felt life sparkle in her blood down to her fingertips.

She dressed, packed a small bag because she intended to stay with Nick for as long as the hospital staff allowed her to, and went downstairs.

Just outside the door, she stopped. Remembering that moment—could it possibly have been only 24 hours ago?—when she came home with Nick. Their first kiss against her door. That feeling of something new and vastly exciting starting. When she looked around her familiar surroundings, it was as if everything became new.

The driver was where she'd left him. He got out and opened the back door for her. "Sorry to take so long," she said.

"No problem at all, ma'am," he answered.

It was late. She'd lost all awareness of time. Today had been endless and it wouldn't end until she was able to see Nick, and if possible, talk to him.

"There are sandwiches and hot tea in a thermos in the bag," the driver said.

Nick, looking after her even from a hospital bed. The arrangements had probably been made by Dylan, but the impetus would have come from Nick.

The crying jag had made her hungry. She opened the container and pulled out a tomato and mozzarella sandwich and poured herself a cup of tea. The container had three types of sandwiches, carrot sticks, grapes and two cannoli. She polished everything off just as they pulled into the hospital parking lot.

To her surprise, the driver got out of the car too. "You don't have to accompany me inside," Parker said.

"Oh, but I do," he answered with a smile. "My instructions are clear. I will accompany you to the floor where Mr. Gardner and Mr. Garin are."

He was smiling, but there was steel visible under the smile, and Parker knew that short of shooting him, too, he was going to accompany her.

He took her small case and Nick's big suitcase as they

walked inside and took the elevator to the third floor. The hospital was silent, with few people around. A nurse came forward, tall, dark-haired, and said "Dr. Donovan?"

Parker nodded and she said, "Follow me, please."

They went down several halls, through a door beyond which was utter quiet. There was only one Marine, standing at attention just outside a door.

The nurse stopped at the door. "Mr. Garin is in here. He came out of anesthesia about half an hour ago, but he is still only semi-conscious." She walked away.

Dylan was sitting in a chair and got up. Parker looked up at Dylan. "Do you think they'd let me stay the night? He might need something."

Dylan smiled. "Parker, I don't think you have quite grasped the situation here. Nick's a hero. You're both heroes. The hospital staff doesn't know any details, nor will they ever, but they do know you and Nick did something extraordinary. Everyone has instructions to bend over backwards to help you."

Parker blinked. She was a *hero!*

Dylan pushed open the hospital room door, and she walked in, and there he was! Nick. Pale beneath his tan, with tubes running in and out of him. Oh God. It took everything she had not to hug him and risk pulling a tube out of him.

There was a chair in the corner. She picked it up and quietly placed it by his bedside and sat down. It was preternaturally quiet except for the beeping of some machine monitoring something. Parker knew nothing about medicine except for the fact she was intensely grateful for modern medicine and Dr. Crowley for keeping Nick alive though he'd been shot.

If Nick had been a legionnaire—no, if Nick had been a Roman in antiquity, he'd have been a *general*—and had had a spear thrust through his abdomen, he'd have probably died. Of blood loss if nothing else. Definitely of septicemia.

But—here he was. Alive. Breathing peacefully. A little dinged, but she'd been assured he'd have a complete recovery.

A miracle.

There was a faint gray tint to the sky outside the window. Dawn was coming. A new dawn, a new day.

It was all ok.

She put her hand over his on the cotton blanket, put her head down next to his and fell fast asleep.

CHAPTER
Thirteen

Pain was there, but somehow far away. *God bless pain meds*, Nick thought. He hurt, but it was as if his body were in another room, together with the pain. Eyes closed, he took stock. He hurt everywhere, but most particularly his shoulder and lower abdomen. There was a reason those two places hurt, but he couldn't actually pinpoint it. Something had happened—something important—but the memory danced just beyond his reach.

He knew where he was. A hospital. No mistaking that smell and the faint sounds of machinery beeping. Nick hated hospitals, but something, some deep knowledge his body had, told him he couldn't simply get up and walk out. He was stuck.

And there was something warm and soft on his hand and something warm and soft and tickly on his face.

With great effort, he cranked his eyes open. Yep. Hospital room. Not light but not dark. He had no idea what time it was or even what day it was. He lifted his hand and found there was something on it.

Parker's hand. Parker's hair, on his face because her head was next to his. She drew in a breath, lifted her head, smiled at him.

She was mussed, pale, without makeup. She was so beautiful.

"Hey," she said.

"Hey." He coughed. His voice came out like a frog's.

"You can have a sip or two of water. Would you like some?"

Considering his throat hurt when he spoke, he just nodded his head. She reached out for a blue thermos, unscrewed the top and put a straw in. She bent the straw to his mouth, and he sucked in blessed, ice-cold water. It felt like heaven. After only a few sips, though, she removed the thermos.

"I was told you can only have a little water at a time, but as often as you like. Don't worry, I'll be here."

He clutched her hand. "What—" his throat seized up.

"What happened?" He nodded.

"Well, in a nutshell, we won. The bad guys came swooping in for the kill, but you shot the first one and I shot the second one after the first one shot you."

His eyes widened.

"Yes indeed. I shot someone. Twice. I hit him, too, because I was highly motivated. He'd just shot you after you ran across the tunnel to shield me. I was so angry. I thought he'd killed you. He was walking toward you with a machine gun held in one hand just like in the movies. But I sighted along that gun you gave me—flipped the safety, red is dead—and aimed for the chest. But then his head exploded and that definitely wasn't me. It was your friend Dylan, who is great, by the way, and the cavalry was right behind him. He'd taken a chopper. So all the bad guys were either killed or taken into custody. And Dylan told me to tell you that no one got a look at us. And no one knows us, knows we were there. And indeed, only three people know we were there. Not even the US soldiers who were there know who we are. Dylan made sure we were shielded."

He blew out a breath of relief. The mob had long memories, and if it was general knowledge that he and Parker had thwarted a major heist of nukes, their lives wouldn't be worth living. They'd have to go into hiding forever.

"What about—" he croaked.

"The nukes? I don't really know, but Dylan said to tell you that NEST is on site and taking care of things. And that you guys don't have to worry anymore."

Nick's shoulders relaxed. NEST officers were among the best and were guaranteed to keep the Davy Crocketts and man portables out of enemy hands. Stateside, the nukes would probably be destroyed.

"Dylan also said that we are never to talk of this to anyone."

Nick felt his eyes widen in horror and he shook his

head violently, then stopped because he had stitches in his neck.

"Don't worry about me. I have no intention of ever saying anything to anyone except you and maybe Dylan. Also—I discovered that I have a violent and bloodthirsty streak I never knew I had, and I'm not proud of it. I have killed a man, and I feel absolutely no remorse. He'd just shot you and I thought you were dead, and I wanted him dead right back."

Nick felt a smile sneak across his face.

Parker looked indignant. "You find that funny?" She stopped, considered. "Maybe it is funny, a little." She squeezed his hand tightly. "I'm so glad you survived," she whispered.

"Glad I survived, too," he whispered.

Parker gave a sly smile. "You know, I saved your life. I think. Or if not, it was a saving-your-life adjacent act. You owe me."

Nick let his eyes roam over that beautiful face. "I do. Big time."

She cocked her head. "How are you going to reward me?"

Well, that was easy. The woman of his dreams had saved his life. How was he going to pay her back?

"Anything you want," he croaked, voice flat. "Anything at all." His voice was weak, but he meant every word with every fiber of his being.

Parker looked startled. She'd been teasing him and wasn't expecting his sober answer. "Oh! Well, what I want is for you to get better. I hate seeing you like this."

He rolled his eyes, and she laughed. "Yes, I know. You hate it more than I do."

There was a soft knock and immediately after Dr. Crowley stepped in, pushing a cart. "Mr. Garin. And Dr. Parker! This is a delightful surprise."

Parker smiled. "Do you want me to leave?"

"That is entirely at Mr. Garin's discretion. Do you want Dr. Parker to leave?"

Nick shook his head no.

Dr. Crowley turned to Parker. "Ordinarily, yes, we'd ask visitors to leave, but it was made clear to me that we are to accommodate the two of you as much as possible." He smiled, pointing a thumb at the ceiling. "Whatever you did, it pleased someone in power. Or several someones. And now, Doctor, I'll have to ask you to move aside."

She stepped aside, back against the wall.

The doctor put on latex gloves and fiddled with things on the cart. Nick did not want to know. He hated being sick, he hated doctors, he hated hospitals. Dr. Crowley held gauze in a forceps-type...thing. He poured a smelly liquid over it. A disinfectant.

"Mr. Garin, can you sit up?"

The fuck kind of question was that? *Of course* he could sit up. Except...he was finding it hard. He placed a hand with an IV line running into it on the bed and pushed, schooling his face to impassivity. It freaking hurt!

So quickly it was over before he realized what she was

doing, Parker stepped forward, put a hand on his uninjured shoulder and pushed and he sat up. Before he thought to tell her he didn't need help, she'd stepped back again against the wall.

The doctor slipped the hospital gown down over his shoulders. "Let's look at the wound," he said.

Nick twisted to see what he was doing. The doctor deftly peeled off thick gauze from his back. Nick had to stretch to see the wound. The wound was as long as his index finger, very neatly stitched up. Didn't look bad at all, and the skin was clear.

Parker gasped.

"It's okay, honey," he said. "It's just a scratch."

"You military types," the doctor said absently, swabbing the wound. It hurt, a little, but Nick would rather be fed to alligators than show anything.

"Not military," he said between clenched teeth.

The doctor stopped, the swab held in the air and stared at him. "You were. You definitely were. I'd bet my degree on it."

Bingo. Nick nodded briefly.

In a moment, the wound was cleaned, together with the wound on his shoulder, and bandaged back up.

Doctor Crowley straightened. "Well, it looks like you're healing nicely. No infection, clean margins. In a couple of days you can go home. Is there anything we can do for you?"

"Yes." Nick put his legs over the edge of the bed. "Can I be released now?"

"Now?"

"Now. I have my clothes." Nick reached for the IV needle in his hand.

Dr. Crowley put his hand over Nick's. It was much smaller than his hand, but sinewy and visibly strong. "Nope," Dr. Crowley said cheerfully. "I know you're used to being the alpha male, but in here, I am. And you stay for as long as I say so. I know you're also King for a Day for something you did that no one can know about, but you do not want to cross me." He smiled. "Trust me on this."

Nick knew when he was beaten. He sighed and pulled his legs back up onto the bed. Parker pursed her lips, trying not to smile.

"Can he eat, doctor?" she asked.

Dr. Crowley was walking out and stopped, one hand on the door, considering. "He's lucky. The bullet didn't hit the intestines. He can eat very bland food. Soon dinner will be served. Cream of wheat and a boiled potato." He shot Nick a smile. "*Buon appetito*," he said, in what even Nick realized was an atrocious accent and disappeared.

Parker approached the bed. She bent and kissed him on the forehead. "It's a good thing I brought you some food, then."

His eyes widened. "You did?"

"I surely did. Food fit for a convalescent, which you are, much as you'd like to deny it, but not food straight from the hospital equivalent of the Consulate kitchen."

"You owe me a home-cooked meal," Nick said, trying to keep a whine out of his voice. They should have had a romantic evening at her place—including food—whereas instead he'd been under anesthesia being stitched up. Though in his heart of hearts, he knew he wasn't up to much today, and it was better to be in bed, hurting, with stitches, than six feet underground. He'd be better tomorrow. He was a fast healer, and he had the best motivation in the world to heal up fast.

That motivation was right by his side, laying out a dinner for him on the table next to the bed.

First, a pretty light green table mat. Then a pretty bowl with flowers around the rim, the flowers matching the color of the table mat. He laughed when he saw what she pulled out next, though laughing freaking hurt.

Silverware. Honest to God silverware made of honest to God silver. They'd been taught to recognize and identify a lot of precious metals.

"A silver spoon? Really?"

She smiled. "I would have set a nice table for you if things had gone normally. Hush now."

He hushed.

Next was a crystal chalice and a glass bottle of sparkling water. "No wine for you, I'm afraid. Sorry."

Then a thermos and she poured out a creamy liquid that was the same light green color as the flowers. Food that matched the décor. That was a new one.

She unfolded with a snap a light green linen tablecloth the size of his desk and put it around his neck and put the solid silver spoon in his hand.

He ate a spoonful of the soup and nearly laughed. It

was absolutely delicious—fresh tasting and somehow minty. And a small slice of focaccia. "What is this?"

She smiled a witch's smile. "I should keep you guessing but you're sick and all, so I won't. Cream of zucchini soup with basil and mint. As easy to digest as cream of wheat but much better tasting."

God yes. He ate the entire bowl and the slice of focaccia. At first, he thought she wasn't serving him much food, but it turned out she'd calculated it perfectly. He was full.

Parker turned to fiddle with the small case and pulled out a small pretty china plate with a small slice of the lemon cake made by her neighbor. And a small silver dessert fork. He wasn't hungry, but he knew first-hand how good that cake was and finished it off.

He was happily stuffed when he sat back while she put everything away. For the first time since the earthquake, he felt...okay. Not great, but okay, and better all the time. Part of it was just the natural healing process of a healthy body, but part of it was her. Parker. Here, by his side.

A reason to get better as fast as he could. He watched her as she put away the dinner things, graceful and smiling. She'd made an extra effort to provide him with better than hospital-quality food and make it an exercise in elegance, something hospitals weren't known for.

She was tired but still looked amazing. Even more alluring than normal because he knew how she got so tired. By trying to help him.

They should have had their evening at her house. Dinner followed by sex all night. They'd missed that. It was a weird feeling to want sex with Parker but not feel warmth in his groin. The burning desire was there, but the blood wasn't pooling between his legs, and he didn't have a hard-on. It would come, just not now.

However, there *was* a pooling of blood in the middle of his chest. Where his heart was, though up until now it wasn't an organ he paid much attention to. Now he was forced to pay attention because he could feel heat, feel it beating in his chest. Like sexual arousal without an erection. Was his heart getting a woodie?

Fuck.

Parker was messing with him without meaning to.

She'd put away his dinner things and pulled a chair to the bed. She sat down and held his hand. It warmed up his entire arm. "What else can I do for you?"

Nick shot her a look, and she laughed.

"Besides that. Down, tiger. Dr. Crowley would definitely not approve. And you've got stitches. There are rules."

Nick gave an exaggerated sigh.

"What's happening with the Consulate? Are you going to continue the contract when you get out? Even if they've caught George, surely there's some mopping up to do? Putting new security features in place?"

"Dylan's taken over the contract. He's a vice president of both Go Solutions and Black Inc. like me. The Consulate's in good hands. He'll put a super secure system in place and figure out what's been compromised."

"Is he as good as you?"

Nick waited a beat. "Yeah."

She laughed again. "Did that hurt?"

He shrugged. "A little."

She cocked her head. "Does that mean you can take some time off? Rest and recover?"

"Oh, yeah," he breathed. Parker Donovan was going to be his personal rehab.

"Good. And I still need to feed you my tiramisu. But only at home, not here. Dr. Crowley would have my head."

Two days later, Nick eased back on Parker's comfortable couch, feet up on a hassock.

Nick had discovered something shocking about himself. He *loved* being pampered. Simply loved it.

Up until now, if you'd asked him, he'd have described himself as a total badass. Tough as they come. Nothing scared him, he could survive anything. He ate nails for breakfast and shat bullets.

That kind of guy.

Instead, he'd fallen face first into Parker's care like falling into a perfumed vat of flower petals. Oh man.

Parker hadn't left his side. He had asked the nurses to put a cot in his room instead of having Parker sleep in an uncomfortable chair and they did. He'd encouraged this with a €200 tip, but that probably wasn't necessary. It had been made clear to him that he could have what he wanted within reason and what he wanted was for Parker to be comfortable, since she refused to go home.

He'd dozed a lot, to his surprise. Just fell right asleep at odd times, only to wake up hours later with Parker right there, usually working on her laptop or reading something on her tablet. As soon as she realized he was awake, she'd put everything down and dedicate herself to making him comfortable. Nick had been wounded before, had had surgery before, but hadn't had Parker by his side before. And man, did it make a difference.

She fussed over him, and instead of it irritating him because goddamit, he was *tough,* he…liked it. Liked her straightening out the bed because God forbid wrinkles in the sheets bother him, holding a glass of water, which she kept chilled in a cooler. Nick drew the line at being fed, but it was a temptation.

After two days of whining, Dr. Crowley finally let him go home. Or to Parker's place, which was better than any home he'd ever had. Parker had a long list of questions about his care and took careful notes.

He'd woken up this morning feeling okay for the first time since he'd been shot, but leaving the hospital, being driven to Parker's place, settling in—it had taxed him, though he'd never admit it.

Parker insisted he sit down on her couch, which was sinfully comfortable, with a very lightweight cotton blanket, and he'd fallen fast asleep.

Fuck. Alone with Parker for the first time since being shot, and he fell asleep.

He woke up and found her beside him, dozing, her head on his shoulder.

Yeah, she'd be exhausted. Sleeping for days on a cot in the hospital, always moving around to make him more comfortable. And though she hadn't been shot or wounded, she'd lived through an earthquake, crawled through rubble and had killed a man.

Enough to make anyone tired.

Nick studied her face as she slept. She had dark circles under her eyes, new lines in her face, and was very pale. She'd never looked more beautiful to him. An extraordinary woman. And his.

Of that he was certain.

She was taking really good care of him. He was going to take really good care of her.

Her eyes opened unexpectedly, wide, tired, beautiful. She sat up, pushing her hair out of her eyes. "Hey," she said. She looked him up and down and seemed satisfied. He hadn't taken another bullet in the time she slept. He was on the mend.

"Hey back."

Parker gave him a soft kiss and stood up. "How about we have dinner at the table, like civilized beings? You must be sick of eating off a tray in the hospital."

"Oh yeah." One thing about his Parker. She liked to live elegantly. Good thing she wasn't a soldier out in the field, shitting in the woods like a bear. But the thing was, Nick loved that about her. Wherever she was, she created beautiful surroundings. Everything she touched became nicer.

Nick stood up on his own, but leaned on her a little as

they made their way to the table. There were candles and pretty napkins and silver napkin rings. Soup in a china tureen—he'd learned the word from Parker—slices of sourdough bread, a small salad. No wine yet, but that would come.

Nick had spent a lot of time, a good portion of his life, in the badlands. Where there was no civilization, where it was dog eat dog and no beauty. He knew where he wanted to be. In Parker's world.

She smiled as he pulled out her chair for her and tried to hide that he sat down heavily in his own chair.

Parker ladled bright yellow soup into his bowl. He leaned over and sniffed. "What's this?"

"Carrot and ginger soup. Full of vitamins for a growing boy."

He laughed and tasted it. It was, of course, delicious. As was the toasted sourdough bread drizzled with olive oil.

When Nick finished the soup and slice of bread, Parker touched his hand. "I have a surprise for you."

"Oh yeah? Am I going to like it?"

"Very definitely. Now close your eyes."

He closed his eyes obediently.

"Open." He opened his eyes and stared at the small serving bowl.

"Ohmygod."

Parker nodded. "I asked Dr. Crowley, and he gave me his okay."

"Tiramisu," Nick said reverently.

"It is. A promise is a promise."

He dug his dessert spoon into the creamy, chocolatey mass and put the spoon in his mouth and closed his eyes. It tasted of heaven. The best tiramisu he'd ever had. He finished the bowl without talking and barely kept himself from scraping the bottom of the bowl for a few more molecules of the dessert.

He picked the bowl up and tilted it to her so she could see just how tragically empty it was.

"Sorry, slick." Parker smiled. "The doctor said one small bowl. But the good news is I have more for tomorrow."

Nick looked over at Parker. She was smiling at him, and he knew that she was doing her very best to please him and care for him. And she was doing a fantastic job. If he played his cards right, this could be forever. He could see her across the table for the rest of his life.

It was what he wanted more than anything in the world.

Nick picked up her hand. He wanted to smile, but it was too big a moment to smile. "Parker Donovan, I've never met anyone like you before. I know we haven't known each other very long, but I know myself and I know I want to be with you forever. Will you marry me?"

She laughed. "For the tiramisu?"

But then she saw that he was serious and stopped smiling. Her hand trembled in his. "Maybe. I don't know what to say. Not many marriages work out."

"Yes. You say yes." Nick startled babbling in a sweat of panic. "But you don't have to say yes immediately. We could—we could live together first. You could get used to the idea. I could definitely relocate Go Solutions headquarters to Rome. Naples would be harder, but Rome could work quite well. You could live in Rome, right? Work in Rome?"

She nodded, eyes huge.

"So we'd live together, see how it works. I think it would work great, don't you?"

Nick picked up her hand, soft and graceful. Everything about her was soft and graceful, and he was astounded at how much he wanted this, wanted it forever. Something of what he felt must have gotten through because she suddenly smiled.

"Probably."

Epilogue

One year later
Villa Serena
Outside Rome

It took him a year to convince her, but he did it. It was finally their wedding day. Nick thought he'd be nervous. Marriage was a big deal. Unless things went really wrong, it was for the rest of your life. But he was fine. Calm. Very sure of what he was doing.

His life had changed beyond recognition anyway. It had been the happiest year of his life. He and Parker had been living together in Rome the past year, in a large apartment he'd bought after selling his flat in London. He'd sold his London flat at a market high and had been able to buy two floors in a palazzo in the center of Rome, one to live in and one as company headquarters. His commute to the office was two minutes. There'd even been money left over to buy his parents a small apartment in the same palazzo.

Parker had made their apartment, his office and his parents' place incredibly elegant. Entering his home, closing the door behind him, Nick always felt better. Relaxed, happy, at peace. And clients were astounded when they entered his headquarters. Security companies weren't known for their beauty.

And Dylan relocated to Rome and loved it.

He'd thought he'd sacrifice business to live with Parker in Rome, but nope. Business went up. Go Solutions was the preeminent security company in the Mediterranean now, where there'd be security work till the sun went nova.

Crazily, Go Solutions had very lucrative ongoing contracts with the Italian Defense Ministry. Parker had accompanied him to a big US Embassy thing they both thought would be boring. As it turned out, the Italian Defense Minister was there, and he was a fan of Roman history and was dazzled by Parker. He and Parker chatted in Latin all evening and the next day Nick was called in for a contract. So far, he'd had ten of them.

Things were going really well for Parker, too. *Apocalypse Then* was climbing the bestseller charts, and the documentary would air in the fall. She was happy and he was happy for her. It was an amazing book and had people buzzing.

"There she is!" someone shouted, and yep, there she was. They were in the villa's garden with silk-covered chairs on the grass, and Parker was walking down the

central aisle. Nick's father had offered to walk her down the aisle—nobody even knew where Parker's father was—but she chose to walk herself to him.

Following tradition, Nick hadn't seen the bridal gown, and he wished he had seen it beforehand because seeing her unexpectedly like that was a blow to the heart. He couldn't tell anyone—not even Parker herself—but sometimes, being with her, seeing her unexpectedly, his heart would give this huge thump in his chest. He even secretly went to a cardiologist once when he was State-side, but it appeared his heart was in perfect working order.

It was his woman who was dangerous.

He couldn't even begin to describe the dress except that it was white, elegant, silk with lace everywhere. She had a lace veil, but he could see through it perfectly and saw when she smiled at him, and he suffered another thump in his chest.

Nick heard a deep sob in the audience, but he didn't have to look to know who it was. His mom. If possible, she loved Parker almost more than he did. She and his dad were spending more and more time in Rome. His mom had found the daughter she'd always wanted, and Parker had found the mother she'd never had.

When his mom was in Rome, she and Parker would disappear for whole afternoons and go on epic shopping sprees. They'd come back with a billion bags, slightly tipsy from drinking Prosecco at Antico Caffè Greco, which they both loved. Parker mainly because, as the oldest café in

Rome, Byron used to drink there. His mom because she liked the Prosecco.

Nick loved seeing both of them so happy and was only annoyed that Parker so rarely made use of his company credit card, paying for everything herself.

A string quartet had been playing, and now they struck up Pachelbel's Canon in B minor, which even he recognized. It accompanied Parker until she slowly reached his side then stopped.

Everything was perfect. Parker and his mom had erected what she called a 'bower' and what he called a lot of flowers. This arch thing that looked like a little slice of heaven. Parker reached for his hand, and he lifted it to his mouth. They turned slightly, both facing Dylan. Who, to Nick's amazement, had gotten some mail-in divinity degree and lately had been calling himself 'The Rev.'

He was going to marry them. Parker loved the idea, so that was that, but Nick secretly thought it was sort of borderline illegal. Dylan was not pastor material.

But there Dylan was, sober, unsmiling, in his best gray silk suit, ready to marry them.

He'd insisted they write their own vows, and Nick had spent sleepless nights trying to write something until he found some words on the internet and shamelessly copied them.

"Dearly beloved," Dylan intoned with a perfectly straight face. "We are here to witness these two united in matrimony. They will speak their vows."

Nick faced Parker. Opened his mouth. And all words

fled from his head. Everything. He'd practiced in front of a mirror endless times, but it was as if his mind had taken a hike.

The silence stretched out.

Someone coughed.

Dylan frowned.

Someone else coughed.

"I love you," Nick finally choked out. And then his throat closed up.

Dylan scowled at him then turned and smiled at Parker. "Parker?"

Parker looked relaxed, more relaxed than him, that was for sure. She smiled up at him.

"Nikolai Alexander Garin. I love you, too. You are the most extraordinary man I ever met. The best man I know. Twenty-four hours after we met, you risked your life for me. Got shot for me. I'm happy when I'm with you and miss you fiercely when you're away. I want to spend the rest of my life with you, loving you. You're the best thing that has ever happened to me. I promise to honor and care for you all the days of our lives, till death do us part."

"Attagirl," Dylan whispered and he pulled out a jewelry bag and out tumbled two rings made of platinum with their names engraved on the inside of the rings. One large and one small. He gave the small one to Nick and the large one to Parker.

Nick took Parker's left hand, with the ginormous diamond engagement ring that she complained about but never took off and slipped on the wedding ring. She took his hand and slipped on his wedding ring, the only piece of jewelry he would ever wear.

"I now pronounce you man and wife," Dylan intoned solemnly then broke out into a huge grin. "You may kiss the bride."

The wedding party broke out in cheers and whistles.

Control yourself, Nick told himself. *You have the rest of your life.* Nick lifted that lacy veil over her face and there she was. The most beautiful woman in the world, and she was all his. He was able to give Parker a sweet, chaste kiss and congratulated himself on his restraint.

Parker smiled up at him, that special smile that always moved him. Because he was the cause of that smile. He was the one to make this beautiful, gifted woman happy.

The wedding party was on its feet, clapping. Someone gave a piercing whistle. Jacob Black whistled like that, but when Nick looked over at him, he was standing there, applauding, an innocent grin on his face.

Well, if ever there was an unlikely avatar of wedded bliss, it was Jacob Black. Incredibly tough and hard, a legendary warrior, and putty in his wife's hands. She was by his side, a beautiful woman, though nothing compared to Parker.

Nick would never say that, though.

Parker stepped forward, bouquet in hand. Subtly, the few single women in the wedding party made their way to the front to try to catch the bouquet.

Nick didn't care who caught it. He was finally married, it was done, and he was going to enjoy the hell out of the rest of his life. He was already thinking ahead to the wedding banquet. Parker had chosen the menu, and it was guaranteed to be spectacular. The huge, flower-strewn table was on the other side of the villa, but Nick thought he could smell the food.

But instead of throwing her bouquet into the crowd, Parker turned and thrust the flowers into Dylan's hands. Dylan didn't surprise easily but he looked utterly aston- ished as he fumbled the flowers.

"Dylan, you're next," Parker said and smiled.

Women of Midnight

Midnight Kiss

Midnight Embrace

Midnight Caress

Her Billionaire Series

Charade

Masquerade

Escapade

Dangerous Passions

Reckless Night

Hot Secrets

Dangerous

Dangerous Lover

Dangerous Passion

Dangerous Secrets

Small Town Romance

Don't Think Twice

Woman on the Run

A Fine Specimen

The Defenders

Protector

Maverick

Fatal Heat

Taken

Runaway

Italian Lovers

The Italian

Murphy's Law

Port of Paradise

The Christmas Angel

Lisa Marie Rice is eternally 30 years old and will never age. She is tall and willowy and beautiful. Men drop at her feet like ripe pears. She has won every major book prize in the world. She is a black belt with advanced degrees in archaeology, nuclear physics, and Tibetan literature. She is a concert pianist. Did I mention her Nobel Prize?

Of course, Lisa Marie Rice is a virtual woman and exists only at the keyboard when writing romantic suspense. She disappears when the monitor winks off.

A small press bound by the belief that every voice matters.

Sign up for our newsletter to learn about new releases and more.
https://oliver-heberbooks.com/subscribe/

Follow us on social media:

facebook.com/oliverheberbooks

instagram.com/oliverheberbooks

amazon.com/oliverheberbooks

youtube.com/@OliverHeberBooksPublisher